THE SINGLE HOUND

BOOKS BY MAY SARTON

POETRY

Encounter in April
Inner Landscape
The Lion and the Rose
The Land of Silence
In Time Like Air
Cloud, Stone, Sun, Vine
A Private Mythology
As Does New Hampshire
A Grain of Mustard Seed
A Durable Fire
Collected Poems, 1930–1973
Selected Poems of May Sarton
(edited by Serena Sue Hilsinger and Lois Byrnes)
Halfway to Silence
Letters from Maine

NOVELS

The Single Hound
The Bridge of Years
Shadow of a Man
A Shower of Summer Days
Faithful Are the Wounds
The Birth of a Grandfather
The Fur Person
The Small Room

Joanna and Ulysses
Mrs. Stevens Hears the Mermaids Singing
Miss Pickthorn and Mr. Hare
The Poet and the Donkey
Kinds of Love
As We Are Now
Crucial Conversations
A Reckoning
Anger
The Magnificent Spinster
The Education of Harriet Hatfield

NONFICTION

I Knew a Phoenix
Plant Dreaming Deep
Journal of a Solitude
A World of Light
The House by the Sea
Recovering: A Journal
At Seventy: A Journal
Writings on Writing
May Sarton—A Self-Portrait

FOR CHILDREN

Punch's Secret
A Walk Through the Woods

THE SINGLE HOUND

By May Sarton

W·W·NORTON & COMPANY
New York London

FIRST PUBLISHED AS A NORTON PAPERBACK 1991

ISBN 0-393-30785-9

PRINTED IN THE UNITED STATES OF AMERICA

W. W. NORTON & COMPANY, INC.
500 FIFTH AVENUE, NEW YORK, N.Y. 10110
W. W. NORTON & COMPANY LTD
10 COPTIC STREET, LONDON WC1A 1PU

1 2 3 4 5 6 7 8 9 0

FOR

GEORGE AND MABEL SARTON

PARENTS OF STRANGE TWINS

'Adventure most unto itself
The soul condemned to be,
Attended by a single hound —
Its own identity.'

EMILY DICKINSON

The quotation above is from 'The Poems of Emily Dickinson,' Centenary Edition, edited by Martha Dickinson Bianchi and Alfred Leete Hampson. Reprinted by permission of Little, Brown & Company.

PRELUDE:

TIME IS A DREAM

PART I

Chapter One

EARLY in the morning between winter and spring, when the grass is frosty, when there is no scent and no sound but a heavy white stillness, and yet you know the blackbird may speak at any moment, a sharp sweet waterfall of sound fall down, and the earth wake — on such a morning the milkman whistles 'Auprès de ma blonde' as he drives down the little alley behind the houses on the Boulevard Léopold. Most of the gardens are secret and forbidding with high walls you cannot see over, but there is one so different from the others that he always slows down when he sees the green hedge in the distance, for perhaps she is there. By five o'clock she is almost always there, sniffing the morning, walking delicately about her domain down the path past the cherry tree, past the three little rosebushes the cards in Alice might have painted, down to the gooseberry bushes. There the path turns beside the strawberries to allow them ten feet of wilderness. The milkman has decided that she is a Russian princess, since it is she who has charmed the swans to cross the park and come to the gate every morning for their crumbs. The milkman has never seen her except at dawn, walking in the garden with her chin lifted, as if she were a little dizzy and it were safer to look up than down.

Sometimes she has a short conversation with a cat. 'Pascal, what have you been doing all night that you look so very sceptical this morning?' Pascal lifts his tiger face to be scratched under the chin. He jerks his thin nervous tail and bounds off into the hedge while she slips into the house through the dining-room door. Both their actions have been accomplished so silently and so secretly that they might be conspirators or ghosts. There is no trace of their passing, not even a footprint in the frost.

If the milkman were ten minutes late and looked up at the house now he would hesitate to whistle, it is so still, with the stillness of a house full of sleeping children. But Doro — for that is her name — is creeping up the stairs; at the long window on the landing she turns and looks down at the garden for a minute, at the cherry tree and the pear tree with their white lime-protected trunks, at the squares of the rose beds. Here she can pause once before the day, the long adventurous day, begins. Here is still the absolute peace and lucidity of the morning, the moment when there is still time for the word that may come (It was on a morning like this that she had written 'In County Cork, Ireland').

At the top of the stairs she takes off the old green burberry and hangs it on a hook in the hall. She never does this without the precise image of Ireland coming to her mind, a particular image, tiny and brilliant like a landscape through the wrong end of opera glasses: she and Annette and Clairette sitting in the impossibly green grass on a raincoat, reading the Comtesse de Noailles and eating bread and butter and apples. She goes along the hall and slips into her room. There are a bundle of blue notebooks to be untied and spread out, the lessons to be prepared. Soon she will be celebrating the death of Patroclus (for the little ones are studying Homer) — a great flaming pyre on the sand by the sea, Achilles cutting off his beautiful hair for his friend. She can never rehearse this lesson without being moved and exalted by the gesture, and as she sits at her desk half-murmuring the words, she might indeed be a Russian princess — for one cannot see that she is only five feet high.

An hour later peals of laughter come from the dining-room. Marthe in the kitchen can hear them, Mamzelle Anne's voice pitched high, towering over the others, giving an occasional shriek. Marthe almost spills the hot milk in her haste to get there before it is over. She adores her demoiselles in their maddest moods. But when she pushes open the door Mamzelle Dorothée is wiping the tears from her eyes; laughter has passed over them like a hurricane and they are exhausted.

'Coffee, Kinder, coffee — I am dying of thirst!' But wicked Mamzelle Anne murmurs as she pours out her cup: 'My dears, he looked exactly like the Père Duval. You'd think I had seduced his son.' The picture of Annette seducing that incredibly fat slow child set them off again.

'Don't! Don't, Annie,' says Doro. 'I am weak with laughing'; and gradually they subside with little sighs, until for a moment there is no sound except the tinkling of the spoons.

Is it time? I'm afraid it is time to say that these are three old ladies. They are called the Little Owls, why nobody knows, but for thirty years they have been called the Little Owls, though nothing could be less like an owl than any one of them, as they are always in bed by nine o'clock. Doro is tiny and delicate, with enormous gray eyes behind dark glasses, which she slips on and off as if she were hiding behind them (and she is), thin fair hair like a boy's, a small strange face that can look very severe when her eyes are hidden. She is a poet.

Claire is the beauty — pigeon-white curly hair, brilliant blue eyes, now always ringed in shadow, delicate hands with a wedding ring on. She is all charm. People say of her, 'She must have been a great flirt.' She loves bonbons, but is not allowed them any more; and silks that rustle, and bows, and flowers on her dresses, but she cannot afford them.

Anne has a lean eager face, bright eyes like a bird's, fuzzy gray hair in a fringe drawn to a knot on top. She is the fun-maker of the family, spirited, intense, quick-tempered — she mothers and cares for the other two with all the swiftness and precaution of a mother bird. She is completely unable to stay still for more than a minute at a time, so now she leaps out of her chair with sudden violence and says, 'Sapristi, what time is it? Those darlings will be tearing up the schoolroom — listen to them!' For the house is not full of sleeping children but all day is full of active, jumping-up-and-down, learning children. She is off! Her entrance into the schoolroom sounds like a revolution, a crescendo of shouts and laughter (for the children adore her), finally subsiding to a steady drone. The battle is on.

Claire and Doro exchange a smile as Claire gets up to let Pascal in. She opens the window with a flourish. 'Mon cher, come and have your milk.' The square of oilcloth is carefully spread for him at his place. He stands between them on his hindlegs, lapping it precisely, one velvet hand on each side of the saucer, while Doro and Claire watch in respectful silence.

'I think his appetite has come back,' says Claire, wiping his chin, and her eyes are just the color of larkspur. This is one of the delicious moments of the day: Doro is thinking to herself: 'Taste it, taste it!' At such moments her heart swells like a bird inside her and she feels quite dizzy with joy. She picks up the big cup of coffee and looks over it at Claire.

'Clairette, what shall we have for supper?' For it is never in a word that the tapestry of their three lives weaves itself closely and delicately, but inch by inch out of the stuff of these moments when nothing is said, when over a cup of coffee in the morning they have looked at each other and felt a little dizzy with joy, so that now after forty years the design is beginning to be apparent, and it is surely a spring scene. Like one of the Flemish tapestries, it is full of unexpected flowers, of rabbits behind bushes, of deer springing out behind thin trees.

It began long ago when Doro was twenty, her first year of teaching. She was just out of school herself. She looked like a frail boy with eyes too big for him. It was whispered in the school that she taught chiefly by reading poetry to her classes. They didn't guess that each of these lessons was a battle against fear (they were many of them older than she) and against the terrible headaches which seized her. They didn't know that at home her mother was dying and that when she left the school at five o'clock it was to go and nurse. They were aware only of the intensity of those unnaturally large eyes (in those days she didn't wear glasses) — of the fire inside that seemed to burn away her voice so that it came out as soft as ashes and they could listen forever. Most of the students were Flemish, girls hoping to get their degree and go out to teach in the villages around Ghent. Of course she was bound sooner or later, amongst them, to discover Clairette.

Clairette was not in any of Doro's classes. But one evening a pupil pointed her out, a tall fair girl in a blue cloak: 'There's Claire. You know, she has had a story published in the *Belgian Review*.' Doro looked at her quietly and then went home without a word. Ever since she was a little girl she had always run away and hidden whenever anything of importance happened to her, so that she could explore it in the secret brilliant light of her mind.

But when someone told Claire that Mademoiselle Latour wrote poetry, she didn't wait an instant. She ran up the stairs, burst in without knocking, and said: 'May I walk home with you? They say you write poetry.' For if Doro withdrew and shut the door upon her joy Claire threw it to whomever would catch, like a rose, and her arms seemed always to be full of roses. No one would ever say no, thought Doro, looking at her violent warm beauty as she stood there that day.

'Where do you live?'

'Rue des Princes. And you?'

'Quai des Moines,' said Doro gravely, as if this were a calamity. 'But I have some errands to do. I'll go in your direction.' She put on her astrakhan cap and worn woollen gloves. Of course it was Doro who went miles out of her way. They had so much to talk about and she didn't feel tired at all. She felt as if someone had bent down and put wings on her little square-toed slippers.

That was the beginning of the long winter. Every evening Claire waited for Doro and then one walked home with the other. Sometimes they went to the park and sat on a bench until their toes were numb. They said very little. But often they wrote each other letters when they got home. It was then that Doro silently, far into the night, brought out word after word and laid them side by side in a pattern. It was then that she suddenly said to herself, 'I am a poet,' as if she had been born again.

Clairette was almost frightened, a little bewildered. When she held Doro's head against hers, the blood in the temples beat so furiously that her fingers tingled afterwards as if they were covered with feathers and blood. She marvelled at their youth and innocence making these abysses, this thunder in the silence. She was almost afraid.

Whereas Doro, as she would do over and over again during her life, was simply swept out as if she had been a boat on an irresistible tide, not looking forward beyond the next day, beyond the next word she would say, beyond the next silence. She was consumed, she who as a child had gone almost blind and spent two months sitting in a dark corner with a little piece of velvet to comfort her hands, who had never breathed to anyone the terrors, the vastness, the glories that lived inside her. Now suddenly here was someone who understood everything, who had read the same books, felt the same things, and who was, as well, everything that she was not, beautiful, a person to whom life would bring gifts one after another and lay them at her feet. No wonder that she simply poured out her heart without thinking.

They were very solemn in those days, the days when pre-Raphaelites were sweeping knickknacks out of Victorian rooms. They were passionately serious like two nuns who had taken vows to love; ridiculously serious, Claire would say now, forty years later. And if she did, Doro would smile her strange secret smile behind her dark glasses and look out of the window at the cherry tree, smiling perhaps at the thought that the blackbird invariably ate all their cherries every year, but it was dear of him to do it because he sang so well in the early morning. Or perhaps she smiled at something else. She smiled perhaps at the absolute violent purity of those two months. For a little while then she had lived, had been able to live in an imaginary world like Fra Angelico's 'Paradise.' She and Clairette shared every feeling, every lightness, every shadow: the world seemed altogether fresh, created for them to walk through hand in hand. They were able to open their hearts to each other, but not for long. It was a world of the imagination and of the heart alone, the heart lifted up to a plane of constant intensity. Looking back she was surprised at her power in those days to do the impossible, to teach all day, to nurse her mother, to walk miles in cold and wet and then after midnight to be writing, writing, writing those pure sharp cries into the silence, those first poems that were so much of dream and so little of earth, that seemed like clouds, like mists and not like words at all.

Meanwhile Clairette was working on her first volume of short stories. She was always, it seemed to Doro, running up the stairs to the classroom three at a time, to bring a letter from Francis Jammes, who had seen in her at once as if the luminous presence of one of his own heroines — Clara d'Ellébeuse or Almaïde d'Etremont. The *Belgian Review* published a story; there was finally the great day when the first volume appeared. Claire moved in an atmosphere of spring, of festival — and of course she fell in love.

Doro was left alone to get through the dark Belgian winter. She began to learn again the silence that her childhood had lived in. Objects took on a curious life of their own at that time. At the moments when she felt afraid of slipping over the edge of sensation, she focussed her attention on the paper-weight on her desk, on the dark red pencil bitten at the end, on the squares of light the curtains made on the ceiling of her room when the lamp was turned out. But there was always the tyranny of her eyes that made the room start turning, turning round her if she looked too long at anything, the beginning of the dizzy spells that were to get worse and worse until ten years later she had to go to bed for a year. Photographs at this time show a very young, worn face, strained like a person suddenly blinded.

She was nineteen. Her father had been dead for ten years, and now after a long gentle illness her mother was dying. Her mother always said, 'My mother was a princess,' and Doro never knew if it was true, but she thought anyone who saw her mother sweeping a room would recognize royalty. Now she was dying, like the daughter of a princess, very gently and gravely. Death could be in no way terrible when it was approached with such graciousness. Her mother seemed small and childlike now, and in the month of March when the blackbird started singing again, she died.

Doro had lived alone in a world of her own since she was a little girl. But this actual physical loneliness was something new. It was something new to come back to the empty room, to know that if one called there would be no answer, and that there was no one in the world whom she had the right to call. She used to lie down when she was frightened and bury her face in her mother's pillow. There, half-suffocated in the warm pillow, she could somehow grasp anguish and by holding it close, make it hers. To possess pain completely seemed one way of conquering it.

The days were so full of teaching and learning to teach that she hardly had time to think. She was beginning to discover her own way of teaching. The atmosphere of her classes was strangely still and intent. She read more than she spoke, reading them all the things she loved best: it was a course in the history of literature. It was an extremely personal affair. These people — Villon, Ronsard, de Musset, Joubert — had been her intimate friends for years. They had comforted and nourished her far better than anyone alive.

She was full of prejudices. She was full of passionate opinions. Her classes were rapt. If they were not, if she noticed the restlessness of inattention, instead of remarking on it she simply withdrew, looked out of the window, and went on for herself until they felt piqued and wanted her back. She was never at any time in her life primarily interested in knowledge. She was interested in revelation, in touching their hearts, these Belgian girls with their wide-apart eyes and flamboyant imaginations waiting to be tapped. How dangerous this autocratic method of her own was she had no idea. She was delighted with the results. She was not surprised or sorry when half of them failed to pass their rigid examinations.

But the director was extremely surprised. Who was the nineteen-year-old teacher who dared to give her pupils themes to write with titles like 'A Bouquet in a Room,' and who had simply cut a third of the prescribed reading? He pulled softly at his moustache as he looked at the sheaf of examinations before him. He would have to speak to her, of course. A bother.

At five o'clock that afternoon Doro put on her jacket with the big revers, retied the bow at her throat with passion, and put on her hat. At last she would be able to speak. It didn't matter at all that she might be dismissed compared to the deliciousness of that, the sense of power it gave her — though her hands were trembling and her head throbbed, sure sign that she was in for one of her terrible headaches.

The director was still looking over the examinations when she came in. For a minute that seemed an eternity he didn't lift his head. When he did, he was startled to be confronted with anyone so small and frail and so very severe. The large gray eyes opposite him didn't waver. He coughed and pulled his moustache, the usual prelude, the comfortable slow beginning of speech. He would have to tell this young lady that she was presumptuous. But Doro had only been waiting for an opening to speak, and before his first word she had already begun, taking off her gloves and laying them on her knees, pulling the fingers one by one, quietly and firmly.

'I know what you are going to say to me, Monsieur. Half of Form B have failed their examinations. I knew of course that they would.'

He laid down the papers. 'But, Mademoiselle...' he said loudly. Doro did not seem to hear. She went on quietly:

'I have come to ask you to read those papers yourself and pass at least half of the failures over the head of the committee. You can do that, of course?' she asked, looking up for the first time and smiling. 'If you read them you will see that those girls have felt and thought and know what they are talking about.'

'Mmmmm. That's all very well, Mademoiselle, but this is a government school and it is just like being in the army. You have been insubordinate, Mademoiselle.'

'I am one of your best teachers, Monsieur.'

'How do you know?'

'I have talent for teaching,' she said simply. She never once would have said, then or later, 'I have talent for writing,' but she was too well aware of the spark that now and then ran from girl to girl until the room blazed with an idea, to doubt that she could teach.

'Yes, you have talent for teaching, that is perfectly true. Let us compromise. I will keep you on if you will try next time to follow the schedule. Combine your talent,' he added with a smile, 'with a little discipline.'

Doro began putting on her gloves. If she compromised now she would have her job. If she didn't — she saw with complete clarity what would happen: borrowing from Clairette, illness.

'I'll try,' she said, and went out without thanking him. That was the first of the battles. Monsieur Duprès was an extraordinary man and long-suffering. Also he had some intimation, for he did read the papers, that she was worth training. He did not foresee that she would be untrainable, intractable, progressively as her confidence increased. Eventually of course she had to go.

But that was years later. Now she was known in the school simply as an eccentric, a poet, and left to her own devices. One is never lonely for very long. Shortly after Clairette's engagement, in March, Anne came to the school and soon attached herself to the two friends, being unable to make up her mind for the rest of her life to which of these two gods her allegiance should be given undivided.

She blew into their lives like a strong salty wind. She immediately adopted Doro, and with infinite tact and finally determination against which nothing could prevail, kidnapped her and brought her back to the big old family house on the Cours des Princes, where she was cherished and nursed and teased tenderly about Clairette, so there was nothing to do but to laugh or cry, and she had done too little of both that winter.

Annette came into their world like a warm and wilful angel and took their lives firmly into her charge. She was as great-hearted as Doro was imaginative, as Claire was *spirituelle*. She was gay; she was unexpected; she was witty, and more than anything she cleared the atmosphere by her very presence. With her arrival the three together made a complete world.

On Thursday afternoons they always met and went for a walk, which usually consisted of skipping arm in arm in the park, then walking back along the quais to the centre of town, where they always made for Vanaise in the Rue du Soleil, who makes the best pastry in the world. There they would sit around a marble-topped table and devour pain-à-la-grecque and those other almost mythological Belgian delicacies. Or they would go to the flower market opposite the château and fill their arms with flowers. On these occasions Annette always kept them in gales of laughter, in the first place by the erratic way she wore her hat, in the second place because it never stayed on for more than a few minutes at a time, and in the third place because when it blew off she laughed till she cried, till they all three had to stagger to a bench to sit down.

It was a relief to Clairette to escape on these afternoons from her personal troubles. There were difficulties in the way of the marriage, family difficulties. Characteristically she had met her young man and decided on the spot that she wanted to marry him. Both families were disturbed by the unexpectedness of this. And he had very little money. But partly owing to Doro's firmness with all the parents the marriage finally took place in April. It was a very cold clear day

— the cherry trees in flower. They were all three there, of course, feeling very sad and very happy all at once.

Doro meanwhile secretly arranged to have a volume of her poems privately printed for Clairette on her birthday. But just as they were finished, when she saw them in print and her own name there for everyone to see and her heart naked inside, she was so terrified at the thought of the parents of her pupils that she withdrew the entire edition and hid it except for three copies for the Owls. When she published again the following year she hid behind a man's name — so she came to be known as Jean Latour.

But the name was not the only reason for having destroyed her first book. It was partly because she felt she had lost that dear silence. She was filled with despair. She wrote: 'Before when people talked around me, I listened, child that I was, and I possessed my thoughts, possessed them alone in rapture and in fear, without wanting to understand or that anyone should understand me. Now I have wanted to say everything. I have stammered. I have dared. And I have said nothing, nothing.'

Perhaps, as she and Clairette sat in the sun finishing their coffee, and she said, 'Clairette, what shall we have for supper?' perhaps it was that whole tapestry of the past that made it unnecessary to speak any more; while out of one glance over the big blue cup another thread went into the complicated pattern of their spring.

'At any rate, let's have cress. I have a longing for bread and butter and cress,' said Clairette.

'But we can't live on cress!' And they laughed, for

it was evident to them both that they could perfectly well live on cress themselves (that was the joke), but of course for Annette they must order a little chicken, which, when it was there, they would both enjoy most frightfully. That was the joke.

Chapter Two

WHEN Doro pushed open the swinging door into the kitchen she found Marthe leaning out of the window with her hands clasped and in a state of what seemed perpetual gasping. 'Oh!' — she caught her breath — 'Oh!' again. Doro ran to the window. 'Marthe, what is happening?' (Had Pascal caught a bird? How dreadful!)

'Oh, Mamzelle, Mamzelle!' — Marthe's sss's were soft and purring with a slight lisp — 'They are putting up the cross on the convent!' The great cross, swaddled in brown quilting, was slowly swinging up over the little tower. All through the fall the building of the convent had been a great source of interest to Marthe, and for that matter to the Little Owls. It faced the Chaussée de Courtrai, but the chapel was at the back in the middle of a garden. The land, they heard, had been willed by the eccentric old Mademoiselle Lepique, whom no one had seen for years, in fact until she was buried.

'Marthe, we must get to work. I have a class at half-past ten, and I must go out to get some cress for Mademoiselle Claire. We should be in peril tonight without cress, it seems! I'll put on my hat while you think what we need. We shall have a little chicken as it is Mademoiselle Anne's birthday, but don't tell!'

'Oh, I won't, Mamzelle.' Like everyone else in this house, Marthe was far from being a plain Belgian girl. Ten years ago when she was just eighteen she had come to Mademoiselle Dorothée, in tears, to explain, as if it were a calamity, that she was marrying the butcher; the butcher turned out to be subject to terrible rages, so one day Marthe came back, in tears once more, to take refuge with her demoiselles. Since then nothing would persuade her to leave the house alone, not even to mail a letter. So Mamzelle Dorothée did all the errands. Luckily there were not many streets to cross before she could get a tram. Beyond about five feet ahead everything disappeared for Doro into a dark mist. But she enjoyed going out. She liked the feeling for a quarter of an hour of being simply an anonymous old lady of whom nothing was expected beyond the power to give the right change to the butcher and the baker. She liked the brisk cheerful greeting of the butcher's wife, giving no quarter to the dream she might have been dreaming, shouting cheerfully, impatiently at her.

'Well, Mademoiselle!'—with 'Wake up!' so definitely in her tone. And of course today was a very special occasion. Today she was getting a fat chicken and a bundle of cress. She was getting cream and (a great extravagance) fresh strawberries from the South of France. And besides, all Annette's favorite things: carrots made of marzipan, a little chocolate violin, three people in '*speculose*,' that special Belgian cookie which tastes like nectar and ambrosia. Doro thought they bore a faint resemblance to the Little Owls, a little fatter, to be sure, and dressed in seventeenth-century costumes they were, but Annette would surely see the resemblance. What else? She considered the piles of pink strawberry bonbons in their glass jar, the piles of hopjes, the rows of chocolates. No, nothing more here.

Now there were three streets to cross, and Doro was so excited and happy that she didn't realize that suddenly the trees and the street and the tall gray houses would start whirling around her. 'The house is on fire!' she said to herself. 'Quick, you are needed!' (These expedients of the mind.) For just a second she hung in the middle of chaos. She stumbled to a tree and leaned against it. 'You must still go to the bazaar, quick, quick!' she said to herself with the world rocking and quaking under her feet. And then once more, by some magic of the will, the slow focussing again, the blur took shape. She sat down quickly on a bench. 'Saved!'

She would sit here a moment. Very occasionally she felt suddenly old, afraid of death, of dying suddenly in the street. 'I've been taming death ever since I can remember,' she said to herself. And sometimes she longed not to make the struggle any more, to let herself slip off. She felt old and ill, and the light burned her eyes. She shut them, remembering that after all it had always been like this. As a child her passion was to run, to run wildly as fast as she could, faster than she could, with always this idea of some peril ahead and behind her, so that when she flung herself against the door at school she used to think, 'If it doesn't open at once I shall die!'

She opened her eyes again. There were the wide cobblestones at her feet and the bark of the tree beside her making a pattern. 'I'm alive. I'm alive,' she thought; and the blood went racing down to her feet and hands so brilliantly, so hotly that her forehead flushed.

Now she must hurry or she would be late for her lesson. To the bazaar! She wanted to get Annette a kaleidoscope, and perhaps, if they only had them, some Japanese flowers. It must all be magic. For this was the birthday of a Little Owl, and to be a Little Owl one must first of all have an essential madness, a special owlish humor, and then one must be a magician. She fairly ran down the street, thinking how peculiar it was to feel as she did and to look as she must, a very pale dull old lady in an old burberry with a felt hat pulled down over her dark glasses. She was once more soaring, carried along on the flood of her imagination. But she would be late, she would be late if she didn't hurry! She fairly flew, and when she got back with the basket full of treasures — the kaleidoscope and the Japanese flowers (even great trees in pots that would fill a whole glass with sea flowers, perfect beauties) — when she got back, she still had half an hour.

'Marthe, you will have to unpack for me. Have you taken Mademoiselle Claire her hot milk? I think she had better have it now.'

Very slowly she crept up the stairs, exhausted after this adventure, letting the rhythm change inside her and the blood beat more slowly, giving herself time, as she stopped at the window on the landing and looked out at the cherry tree, giving herself time to prepare her mind for a concentrated deep effort. Always, every single day, she approached her lessons with awe and expectation and, though it is a word she would hesitate to use, a sense of glory.

In the blue room upstairs there were cupboards full of notebooks written and rewritten, the barriers of imagination without which she sometimes thought she would not know where to find succor. And she found herself turning to them more and more, and away from the world of war which she understood so little and which filled her with horror. From a summit called Shakespeare or Chartres Cathedral or Molière or Tolstoy she saw, she understood, she chose perspectives of splendor, of courage, of heroism — and sometimes she felt that that alone made it possible for her to speak, as her work in the world was to teach.

She took off her coat and hat slowly and thoughtfully. She pushed open the door into her room and looked once at each object, the photographs, the paintings, gathering herself up for the task, for the adventure of the morning.

Meanwhile downstairs in the schoolroom Annette was carrying on a battle with the imperfect subjunctive. She had the power of making the children feel that everything was challenge, that they were taking part in each class in a drama of heroic proportions — except when suddenly her infallible sense of humor sent a wave of laughter over the schoolroom. Her classes were run at a great pitch of excitement — she scolded and embraced the children passionately, and managed with the greatest charm to thrust down their throats the sums and grammar and history and biology that they had to know for their examinations. Owing to her special genius the school had a high reputation as preparation for the university, and she was justly proud of her pupils' records at examination. For with all her impetuousness she could be angelically patient with a slow child, with a difficult child, and, characteristically, loved these always the best.

Across the hall, Doro's class was a different world. Her courses, devoted to art and literature, kept her blessedly free from the tyranny of examinations. She could afford to teach only what interested her, what would be able to be built permanently into the children's hearts and minds. On the walls she had pinned reproductions of Botticelli, Fra Angelico, Manet, two or three Japanese prints. The children entered this room quietly. They stood in little groups. They were just a little afraid of Mademoiselle Latour, who never scolded or embraced them like Didi (as they called Annette), who seemed surrounded with mystery, slipping into the room silently with her hands in the pockets of her jacket, speaking so softly: 'Good morning, Jeanne. Good morning, children,' speaking with a curious respect as if they were grown up. Sometimes they would be told to be very quiet, and they knew that somewhere in the mysterious 'upstairs' that they never saw, Mademoiselle was fighting one of her terrible headaches.

At home they heard her spoken of as a poet. Their parents came back from her public lectures quite in awe of Mademoiselle Latour themselves. In Belgium, and particularly in a small city like Ghent, these 'femmes de lettres' are apt to become legends, and Mademoiselle Dorothée, who never went out, was certainly a legend. The rare occasions when she spoke in public were remembered long afterwards — her plea at the founding of the experimental theatre, her speech at Verhaeren's death, her speech of acceptance at the Belgian Academy 'In Praise of Poetry.' Something of what she called 'glory' came in the door with Mademoiselle Dorothée. The class always stood. They stood because it would have seemed wrong not to, and they could not have explained exactly why. It had become a tradition to stand. There were no longer any children in the class who remembered Mademoiselle's few words of explanation when once a new child did not stand. She said then: 'You are not standing in my honor, you know. But we are standing here together in honor of the beautiful things I am going to read you.' And after the class she asked the child to come up to her room and gave her a post card of Tobias and the angel, and said that the angel would tell her why she must stand. The child thought it a little strange, but she often looked at the card. She wondered a great deal. It was this capacity for exciting wonder that made Doro's classes extraordinary, for she did not seem to teach. She did not explain. She created an atmosphere by her very presence, and then gave them one by one the words she had brought with her. 'If they don't wholly understand,' she said, 'it doesn't matter. They will remember something else.' She said, 'Don't try to remember what I am reading. Try to feel it.'

So now she looked very severe and sad as she began to read of the burial of Patroclus in the *Iliad.* How magnificent it was! As she read, seeming herself completely absorbed in what she was doing, hardly looking at the class, taking the dark glasses off with her restless right hand and then putting them on again as if this continual gesture marked the rhythm of her thoughts, as she read in that soft grave voice, forgetting them, it seemed, entirely, the children slipped off one by one into a dream of their own. The words ran over their heads like water. They felt as if they were dreaming 'Oh, give us day' — that had a nice sound. The little girl with the pigtails in the corner was drawing a camel and thinking 'Oh, give us day.' But the soft voice was going on, and, without ever being raised was, they felt, carried along on a stream of rising emotion. They began to get a little sleepy, a little restless.

At this moment there was the sound of the front door banging and a frightened wail, followed by the excited barking of a dog. Doro got up and went out. There in the hall was one of the littlest ones — she did not take the English lesson and had been sent out to play. Now she was standing at the far end of the hall hiding her head and hiccoughing with sobs.

'Where is Didi?' she said. 'Where is Didi?'

'Didi is busy. What is it? Were you frightened by the dog?' She nodded and pulled a handkerchief out of her bloomer leg. Doro was at a loss.

'Would you like to hear something very beautiful?' she said, putting one hand hesitantly on her shoulder. 'Or would you rather just stay here and drink a glass of water?' She went into the kitchen, and Marthe saw at once that something terrible had happened. 'A glass of water, Marthe. There is a child crying in the hall.' It all seemed so unnecessary. There was too much anguish already without adding to it.

The child took the glass in her two hands and didn't look up. 'Come,' said Doro, 'it doesn't matter if you cry in there. It is a very sad poem I am going to read. You can cry as much as you like,' she said. The child looked terrified and shook her head. 'What is your name?' said Doro.

'Marie.'

'Well, Marie, I think it would be very brave of you to come with me'; and of course there was nothing to do but go, though she was hiccoughing most frightfully. But Doro had her own way of making peace, and she was sure that a poem was the thing.

'The poem is by Victor Hugo,' she said quietly as she came in with a little hiccoughing creature in a white apron. 'Doudouce, is there room beside you for Marie?'

Demain, dès l'aube, à l'heure où blanchit la campagne,
je partirai.
Vois-tu, je sais que tu m'attends!
J'irai par la forêt, j'irai par la montagne.
Je ne puis demeurer loin de toi plus longtemps.

Je marcherai, les yeux fixés sur mes pensées,
Sans rien voir au dehors, sans entendre aucun bruit,
Seul, inconnu, le dos courbé, les mains croisées,
Triste, et le jour pour moi sera comme la nuit.

Je ne regarderai ni l'or du soir qui tombe,
Ni les voiles au loin descendant vers harfleur
Et quand j'arriverai je mettrai sur ta tombe
Ce bouquet de houx vert et des bruyères en fleur.

As she finished, her chin lifted with that curious aloofness they knew so well and a kind of pride they felt and did not understand. In the silence that followed, something like a cry, a great unsatisfied desire once more cherished and then set free like a bird, flew out of the window. The sharp bell of the recess rang. Immediately chaos filled the room, books being slammed down, restless bodies eager to move, loud voices glad to be released from the hush.

'Good-bye, children.'

When they were all gone Doro took a step down from the platform and went over to Marie, who was sitting there feeling terrified, feeling strange, too much happening all at once.

'Well, how did you like it, Marie?' Marie looked at her once from under her lids, nodded quickly, and blushed. She wanted to get away. Besides, Didi would be wondering where she was.

'We'd better go and find Didi — she might think you were lost.' Just then Didi herself burst into the room. 'Ah, there you are, Marie. What is it? What has happened to you?' Marie ran and hid her face in Didi's dress. 'There, there, run along, pussy. Tomorrow you can visit the English class like a grown-up child,' she added. Marie made her escape. 'You know, Doro, she is a darling, that child.'

'She was frightened by that nasty little dog of the Morels' — they should keep it in.'

Doro felt very tired. 'I am going upstairs for a few minutes before lunch.' She turned at the door. 'Don't go into the dining-room, whatever happens, until the bell rings.'

'I won't; I won't. Besides, I have to talk to that Duprès woman, she thinks Albert is overworked — fat, lazy little thing that he is. Ouf!' And in spite of these harsh words Doro knew perfectly well that she would take infinite pains with the 'Duprès woman' and manage to make her understand perfectly what was the matter.

'Bonne chance!' Doro went softly up the stairs to Clairette's door.

'Clairette, Clairette, life is a difficult business,' she said, sitting down on the flowered cushions on the bench in the corner. Clairette's room was the most feminine in the house, gay, with flowers and a little blue virgin in the corner. She was writing at her desk.

'Yes, I heard some sort of drama going on this morning. I couldn't hear myself think.'

'That poor little Marie was terrified by the Morels' dog — Annie is so marvellous with the little children. I always feel at a loss — Yes, I am altogether mad, a poet with no idea of what life's all about,' she said, and at once they were Owls again — a certain word, a certain inflection and they were off on the game, the point being never to take life seriously. And as if to announce that the curtain was up and the play must begin, just at that moment Marthe knocked and came in all red in the face in the greatest agitation and said: 'Everything is on the table, but Mamzelle is still talking to that lady in the hall. What shall I do? Who is going to carve the chicken?'

'Who is going to carve the chicken?' said Claire solemnly, so solemnly that Marthe looked quite frightened for a minute. 'You know we cannot possibly have it, because anyone of us would be liable to cut off a finger if we attempted so difficult a feat.'

'Marthe, you will have to do it. Ring the bell, and

we shall simply sweep Madame Whatever-her-name-is out!'

'All right, Mamzelle,' said Marthe, beaming. Her demoiselles had gone temporarily mad again and she was delighted. Caught up in the general folly, she got out the great gong that they never used and beat on it with a spoon, so that Madame Whatever-her-name-is could not hear herself speak for several minutes and was forcibly reminded that it must be time to leave.

Chapter Three

THE dining-room furniture had all come from Clairette's house, and it gave the little room a patriarchal appearance which delighted the peacocks. Whenever Doro came in and stopped at the threshold to look over at the heavy carved sideboard with the 'Famille Rose' bowl on it, the photographs of Claire's parents in their garden, Pierrot's sketches of the South of France, when she saw their three chairs drawn up around the table and today the pile of packages at Annette's place, she thought, 'This is our house.' And when she looked out of the great door that opened right into the garden which was an orchard as well she thought, 'This is our garden,' and it seemed extraordinary that it could be true.

Annie burst into the room waving a letter just as Marthe was laying down the fat golden bird on its *canapé* of cress.

'Where is Clairette? Look what the Chéri has brought me' (in Owl language the postman was the Chéri) — 'a letter from Percival! Call Clairette quickly, I'm so hungry I shall fall over the chairs! Oh! Oh!' (Her eyes fell on the pile of bonbons at her place.) 'I am in such a state of turbulence that I shall start trumpeting, my darling. What is all this?' Annette was irresistibly swept upon a tide of alliteration whenever she tried to say more than a few words: extraordinary images leapt into her mind, and in the excitement of the moment became mixed so that her sentences were extremely picturesque. She said 'Mon Dieu, I could drop into a teacup.' By this time Doro was already weak with laughing and Clairette, who was just coming in with a bunch of anemones tied with a bright red ribbon, was greeted vociferously.

'Look at her; she looks like an angel! My dear, you had better go upstairs. This is too ribald a gathering for you. Look, her eyes are positively seraphic. Your eyes are too blue to be a Little Owl. You are altogether too good,' said Doro, running up and standing in the doorway with one arm round her.

'Happy birthday, Annette,' they said together, and bowed like Tweedledum and Tweedledee. 'And now, children, we must eat or we shall die of hunger before reading Percy's letter. You know, Clairette, there is a letter from Percival,' Doro said as they sat down.

'Put them in a glass, you putterer.' Annette took the anemones with the brusqueness which was the mark of her emotion. 'Oh, Clairette, my favorite flower!' she said, running over and enveloping Clairette in a hug.

Percival deserves a place here because it was he who invented the Little Owls. Years and years ago at the flower fête in Grasse in the Midi (it sounds like the beginning of a fairy tale), at about seven one evening, Clairette was making her way in the rain to the hotel where she was staying with her family. She was about twenty. She had no umbrella. Suddenly out of the night an incredibly long thin boy in vermilion felt slippers with rosettes of white roses on them and holding a large umbrella full of holes about four feet over her head — suddenly this extraordinary figure appeared and said, 'If you will allow me, Mademoiselle,' and offered her his arm. One of the rules of the fête is that you cannot insult anyone. Differences of class, of wealth, of position must be forgotten. Claire said: 'Thank you very much, Monsieur. I admire your shoes, but how do you keep them clean?'

'Oh, I fly, you know. I never walk at all — just now, for your sake, Mademoiselle, and because you resemble so much Botticelli's "Primavera," I am holding my feet to the ground by an extraordinary effort of will.' By the time they reached the hotel, friendship was established on a firm basis.

The next autumn he came to Ghent on a visit, and immediately christened the trio 'the Little Owls.' Percy is now the well-known French novelist Percival Sauveur. But at the time when the Little Owls first knew him he was a completely fantastic character. He was immensely tall and thin. He had blue eyes. He was ingenuous, imaginative, a little mad, and, like everyone else, in love with Clairette — an Owl, in a word.

It was at the time when Annie had kidnapped Doro and Doro lived with her family in the famous 'blue room.' The blue room, wrote Percy, was deliciously blue. Japanese prints, embroidered silks, water colors by Pierre Van der Ghinst, the peacock's friend, decorated it. There were Flemish pieces of furniture dark and polished; on the mantelpiece a boxwood owl turned his head away when you touched him; on a huge table lay embroideries in progress, dolls' clothes, boxes, paper, cigarettes, a paradoxical heap of tiny, brilliant objects, amusing to look at, soft to touch — and not a grain of dust. Blue cretonnes and blue wallpaper radiated such a subtle atmosphere that it seemed as if it was always the color of the weather, the color of beautiful weather, which it was not outside, which it was absolutely pointless for it to be outside since the Owls had no desire to leave this marvellous room.

They drank tea; they read poetry, they told Belgian stories, they drank more tea. But can you, reader avid of adventure, can you understand all this which has charm only for ingenuous souls, loving Nietzsche as well as Saint Francis, with the same innocence, liking Walter Crane's water-colors, the conversation of beggars, Waldteufel's waltzes, nonsense, silence, and nothing — Little Owls, in a word?

Percy sat cross-legged on the floor of the blue room embroidering borders on their ties. 'A little point of vermilion, Clairette, what do you think? A dot on top of each of these triangles' — or he would make chasubles for his tortoise Agathe, who travelled everywhere with him in a Japanese box.

When they went out arm in arm to look for 'fouffes,' little pieces of silk, or to bring back a wonderful tea, they sang in the street, did imitations of the people they saw, and altogether behaved shockingly. On these occasions Annette's hat blew off every five minutes, always escaping the canal by a miracle, and leaving them at the end of the chase exhausted with laughing.

Then they would come home and talk half the night or invent sentimental tunes to one of Doro's poems, sing them to a waltz, until finally Annie (who, having spent three times the energy of the others in recapturing her hat, was proportionately exhausted) would solemnly announce: 'Agathe is saying her prayers'— evidently a suggestion that they all go to bed.

Amongst other things Percy was famous for his collection of dolls. Whenever Doro looked back on the war now it was always (perhaps deliberately, because the war was a useless thing to look back on) through the eyes of the old Professor. For four years, of course, the Little Owls never saw Percy, so he had sent the Professor to take care of them. The Professor looked like Benjamin Franklin except for his whimsical expression, and except for the fact that his hat played 'Malbrouk s'en va-t-en guerre' when he lifted it to a lady, a rather incongruous performance but full of charm. All through the war, while the Little Owls got thinner and thinner and more wan, the dear Professor looked whimsically at them, lifted his hat, and tinkled 'Malbrouk s'en va-t-en guerre'; it was very comforting. At night when Clairette had slipped home and Anne had gone to bed, when the Professor and Doro were left alone in the blue room, he used to sit opposite her at the desk while she wrote his impressions of Belgium in 'The Diary of the Professor.' It was very quiet at night except for an occasional rumble, an occasional sharp explosion far away, and the regular click of the guard going by at intervals to remind one that liberty was an illusion. Doro would run her hand through her hair and write 'Eight hundred and tenth day of the war.' She and the Professor waited for the third member of these nightly reunions. The third member was neither a real person of leather and sawdust like the Professor nor an unreal mystery of flesh and blood like Doro — he was a spirit. His name was 'Chut,' and he was that dear silence. Once he had come Doro would sigh as if released from some terror, and pick up her pen. Then in a pink notebook such as children use she wrote, looking up now and then affectionately at the Professor to be sure she understood him. Somewhere in the diary, which still exists folded away in a cupboard among the piles of notebooks, there is this description of herself. The Professor is writing to Peter, another of the dolls:

'Well, my dear Peter, Dorothée looks like an old maid. She is a little strange and disconcerting at first sight. You might not like her at all, you who have married an Oriental beauty. But I am a French scholar, a philosopher, and a wise man; I am not much concerned with mere exterior beauty. It's all the same to me that Dorothée is neither young nor pretty. I like her huge eyes, so attentive to my well-being, her tiny dry hands, which lightly and adroitly make a sort of snowstorm around us of books, little objects, work-baskets, pens — and then stop all at once, folded together, as if there were nothing to do, nothing more to do in the world but wait for it to end without lifting a little finger! I even like her thin hair cut short (which I hated the first day, it is so lacking in elegance for a woman), her long nose, her unfinished eyebrows, and her slightly pointed ears! Why not admit it, Dorothée is ugly, but after all, am I beautiful? And besides, never mind; I like her as she is!'

In Ghent twenty years later the atmosphere had changed very little — the shouts of laughter over the hunt and final discovery of the wishbone, the teasing, the gales of laughter, the tying of Annette's red bow from the flowers around Pascal's neck, and his mistress's abject apologies for laughing, all might have taken place in the blue room. And even more so when it came to the moment to open Percy's letter. It was greeted with an 'Oh, let me see!' from Clairette, and snatched out of Annette's hands by Doro, for he had discovered one of those fantastic pieces of letter paper bordered with flowers and gilt scrolls which is used in Belgium for New Year letters. This had a pale blue border with spring green leaves and very pink roses all outlined in gold.

'Read it aloud, Doro!'

'Wait, wait!' Annette waved her arms like a windmill as if to ward off a torrent of words, a declamation, instead of Doro's soft voice, 'Wait, the Prince is waiting at the window to be let in.'

'Oh, my beautiful!' Clairette got up. It is a pity to have to admit in the interests of truth that Pascal was one of the commoner varieties of cat. But there is no doubt that he was a philosopher, and after all the peacocks recognized spirit before matter. Besides, they always affirmed that he had an Egyptian face and was fit to be worshipped. So the window was opened most tenderly for him before Percy's letter could be read.

'Dear and august Little Owls, your humble servant wishes once more to remark, as you have probably forgotten, that this is a great and noble occasion. He is referring not, as you with your usual rapidity of intellect have inferred, to the birthday of its most distinguished because maddest member known as Annette, but to the fact that on this day, thirty years ago in the middle of the Avenue Louise in Brussels, as His Majesty the late Leopold II was passing on his horse, the aforesaid Annette, in an effort to recapture her hat, ran into a tree, and emitted such extraordinary sounds as a consequence that his late Majesty turned on his horse and (a reliable witness attests) smiled for the only recorded time during his reign.'

At this point Marthe came in to clear away. In the excitement the cress had been entirely devoured and the remains of the chicken lay mournfully on a naked platter.

'Oh, Mamzelle,' said Marthe, beaming on them from the great distance of her superior sanity, 'you have left half the chicken.'

'Yes, it is a pity,' said Anne, looking contemplatively at it.

'But,' added Doro, 'we are saving our thirst for the pear.' (There is a Belgian proverb which advises one to save one's pear for one's thirst. But the Little Owls always turned proverbs around to celebrate pleasure rather than virtue.) 'There are strawberries coming!'

'Les fraises et les framboises,' sang Annette.

'I wonder,' said Claire thoughtfully, 'if the neighbors think we drink.'

'Probably,' said Doro. 'Oh, children, we have forgotten our tonic!' Anne leaped out of her chair to get the big black bottle, the three glasses, and the spoons. One day they had looked at each other, and they all three looked so pale and old and sad that they burst out laughing and decided that something must be done. So they had started taking this extraordinary tonic which, if it did nothing to their weak hearts and fragile bones, did wonders to their imaginations. The week of the beginning of the taking of the tonic they all accomplished great feats and ran up and down the stairs. But by now in March, the power of the imagination was beginning to wear off. It was time, they thought, for spring instead of tonic. But it had become a solemn rite, and must be taken very seriously at every meal just the same.

'How have we managed to get through this meal without our tonic?' said Clairette, looking with wide innocent very blue eyes at Doro. 'Do you feel all right, Doro? Do you feel all right, Anne?'

'Let us pretend that we have taken it,' said Anne. 'I am sick of tonic,' she said, and waved the bottle in the air. 'Going, going, gone!' and she closed the door of the sideboard on it. 'I'm sure strawberries are far far better for us. Let us have them every day. We are sure to get pinker and pinker.'

Claire took a silver case from her pocket and lit a cigarette. On special occasions she smoked one after lunch as well as one after dinner. A little silence fell on them in the silence of the smoke curling up over their heads in a blue spiral. They felt, each in her own way, that the winter was long this year, and each in her own way felt a little sad, a little diminished. Clairette's thoughts wandered like white butterflies, resting first here and then there, and finally settling on a really very embarrassing thing that had happened to her.

'You know how absent-minded I am,' she said with a twinkle in her eye. 'Well, just imagine what happened to me. On my way to church last week an old woman came towards me with her hand outstretched and I shook it warmly, wondering while I did it who in heaven's name she was. It was the old beggar who is always there. The poor thing was simply delighted, and rushes up to shake my hand every morning. I feel like those ostentatiously practising Christians. It is really awful, you know. What am I going to do?'

'Well,' said Annette thoughtfully, 'to be consistent, of course, you had better shake hands with every beggar you meet. I don't know how otherwise you are going to satisfy your conscience, Claire. I really don't!'

But they were tired all three, so this sally was greeted simply with a quiet appreciative smile from Clairette, who blew a puff of smoke in Annette's face. They were always teasing Claire gently about her late embracing of the church. 'Let us go up together,' said Doro, taking her arm. They stopped for a moment on the landing and looked down at the garden.

'I wish the blackbird would come back,' said Doro.

Chapter Four

DORO pushed open the door into her study, the room which looked onto the garden where the books stood on their low shelves, where the walls were brilliant with many small paintings one above the other, where above all the cherry tree outside the window seemed like a constant benevolent presence. Doro went to the window, picked a geranium leaf from the pot on the sill, pressed it in her fingers, and smelled it for a long moment as she looked out.

Every day she regretted that this precious hour of peace in the afternoon always found her now torpid from head to foot so that when she tried to shake the dust from her thoughts they simply fled and left her empty, deserted, distracted. There was simply nothing to do but go back and wake some sharp precise memory and rest in it for a little while. So when she took the geranium in her hands and crushed it she drank in the strong pungence, the savor of certain summers long ago. Was this getting old, this devouring sense of the past which looked so often blurred and then suddenly stood out distinct as if her eyes could only focus there? Was this not growing old but simply living after all? Was this life? This slow penetration of experience until nothing had been left untasted, unexplored, unused —

until the whole of one's life became a fabric, a tapestry with a pattern? She could not see the pattern yet.

With the geranium in her hand she saw only certain images: herself sitting in the grass near Fontainebleau with Pierre and Bird and his wife; the smell of grass; Jeanne taking sandwiches out of a hamper and talking noisily; her own silence, looking far off into the light, and then Bird turning on her his too-penetrating blue eyes and saying very gently:

'Miss Dorothy, it is time I rolled you a cigarette.' He always called her Miss Dorothy, and his slight French accent gave it a special charm. When they said 'Bonsoir' he always added 'Good night, Miss Dorothy,' for his father had been English.

Sometimes he and Pierre painted all day. It was just at the time of the impressionist revolution, and they were in the thick of it, setting one tiny brilliant point of color beside another, catching the color of air and the color of light in a multitudinous iridescence. Doro sat in the grass doing nothing, saying nothing, but painting over and over again in her thoughts that slight English-looking figure with his white hair and astonishing young golden beard, his too-blue eyes that saw everything, that knew of course that she loved him. The cigarettes always came unrolled and she could not smoke them at all. Then he would smile his gentle amused smile and make her another, call her back from the too painful dream with another present of black tobacco in a little white paper as if to say: 'All right, poet. Go off on your dream, but don't forget to come back.'

Jeanne had been his model. He married her after living with her for two years, married her out of the courtliness of his nature, and now imposed without a word in the gentlest way an absolute respect for her from his friends. He had married her out of gentleness and not out of love, and now this gentleness imposed silence on Dorothée and on him. What he felt she never knew. She never tried to guess. This love was an abyss into which she cast her poems one by one, like petals to be carried down into a deepness of which she would never see the bottom. She had hidden her first poems so that no one could buy them. Then she published a series of slim volumes only in order to be able to send him the first copy without dedication, which he answered always with a brief note that was more like silence than a word.

Bird died when he was fifty-five, just six years after she had first known him, and the silence which had seemed golden while he lived became bitter as ash now that nothing could ever be said that he would hear and no poem written that he would see. Even here with the geranium bringing pungence and a sweet strange savor into the day she had to get up and go, flee into the other room, the bare little bedroom with the work waiting, to escape the horror of that silence of Bird's death. It was that silence that had been in the room after she read Hugo's poem, that had made the children suddenly restless. It was that silence that had given her mouth its bitter shutness as if it had closed on a cry of anguish that must not be heard.

Here, sitting at her desk, she was safe. Here was a different silence, a different solitude, the solitude and silence of work, of living, of all the energetic demands that living made on her. Outside, sun and wind. Here, the photos on the mantelpiece, the little bottles of ink, the blue notebooks. She picked up her pen and a large sheet of white lined paper and wrote.

It was a single word that made her write, suddenly write a poem though she had been so tired: it was the smell of geranium leaf and the word, a commonplace word, an old word charged with memory, bringing with it a freight of sensation — a little word that seemed to have no significance and yet the word of all the words in the world that could make her write this poem. The word was 'grass,' and with it, as if nothing could possibly separate them, 'tender,' not brilliant, not pungent but tender, and with it all the associations of those iridescent days. As she said it 'iridescent' took its place like color on a palette, and 'tender,' which a moment ago had seemed the only word in the world, was crossed out with a firm stroke of the pen.

> The iridescent grass, the timeless color,
> The warm remembered smell out of the past,
> The light too brilliant on your pallor,
> These are the things death numbs us from at last.

The poem is untranslatable, of course, but when she made it, though she saw at once that it was not a good poem, and that between that electric current the word had set burning and the pen and the paper something had happened — still, when she had finished and blotted it on the blue blotter she felt elated, prepared, and in some way distinguished. Here was an accomplished fact, the tangible picture of her mind, however clumsy. And Jean Latour, our dearest poet in Belgium, closed the ink bottle, thinking to herself, 'I wish I were a poet, a real poet.'

Poetry had always been her little sister and her mother and also sometimes — at the times when she herself became a poet — the white clown as Watteau painted him with long white sleeves, his hands hidden under him, with a round white hat on the back of his head binding the curious, impassive, sad, aware face as if it were a mask.

She had seen him for the first time riding all night in a third-class railway carriage from Paris to Brussels. It was after her first meeting with Bird at Pierre's studio, when in a flash she had seen as well the end and the beginning all at once very clearly, as one does on a night journey in a third-class railway carriage. 'It was,' as she said in her first book, 'early, early in the morning. I was coming back from Paris. It was the moment when one is jolted awake, just as the sky begins to lighten, at the moment when one shivers. The train lurches, the express train, the return train.' She had looked out and seen something white in a field lying asleep, and she said to herself that it was Watteau's 'Gilles,' the white clown that looks like an innocent. And in the early morning because she was so cold and so sad, and because she had seen Bird and the clown at the Louvre, she began to sing very softly to herself the old lullaby that her mother used to sing:

'Fais dodo, Colas, mon p'tit frère,
Fais dodo, t'auras du lolo,'

over and over again until she fell asleep. After that the clown became her muse. She felt they were both sad in the same way, and she liked to pretend that she had really seen him. Sometimes the things one imagines take on a life of their own almost without one's will. It had been like that with the Gilles. He appeared somewhere in almost every one of her books as if by accident, or coincidence.

Meanwhile in the other rooms of the house a tremendous amount was going on. In the kitchen Marthe had been in the midst of polishing the copper pots that hung over the stove, making it look like an altar. They stood around her now in a gleaming golden and bronze circle while she picked them up one after another, admonishing them, as she rubbed their necks and fat bellies, to try to keep a little cleaner in the future. She was sitting back to the window, which meant that she had to get up every few minutes to see how the cross on the convent was getting along. They had already unwrapped it and Marthe couldn't believe, it looked so small, that it could be that giant bundle she had seen four men lift and attach to the hook that bore it up. Now there were two men, one on each side. They had been there for hours doing something at the base. And to Marthe's great disappointment they were now taking time out for lunch, sitting on the platform at the base and swinging their legs. She thought it rather rude of them to swing their legs and spit from the shadow of the cross, but she looked at them a little wistfully as well and wondered if their socks needed mending. It was all very well to work for her demoiselles all day and even die for them, but nothing after all could replace a man once work was done. If only her Albert had not been such a drunkard! Ah, well, it was God's will, no doubt. God's will she always imagined as a great golden writing in the sky like the aeroplane writing she had seen, advertising rat poison, to be sure. But she could very well imagine God's having written one day after serious consideration of the problem, 'Marthe had better not marry again.' Besides, what would become of her demoiselles? Perhaps He had even had that in mind when He wrote what He did. So she took a last look at the handsome mason swinging his legs under the cross, and went back to her blue chair and to the waiting circle of copper pots.

In her room Annette was sitting at the desk with a sheaf of little papers spread out around her, struggling with the accounts. At sixty her days were still so full that this was the way she rested after her morning's teaching. There should be some means, she thought, of mastering the accounts once and for all — why was it that there was always an unexpected bill, that though their lives never changed during months and years, still one month the bill for meat would seem formidable, another month the gas bill would suddenly assume extraordinary proportions? It was one more proof of her energy and devotion that Anne had insisted on running the house as well as taking on the greatest number of hours of teaching. For it is I, she thought happily, who am like the root of this tree. She wondered with a smile if they would not all three just blow away one night if one of them were not well embedded in the solid earth. She thought with so much tenderness and warm active love of her two friends that she must eternally and every day find new ways of proving it. For they were two innocents, she thought, who must be guarded and protected from all material worry: they were two darling geniuses, and it was her business to keep them from harm, to see that a hot-water bottle found its way into Doro's bed, to see that Claire's silk bed-jacket went to the cleaners and reappeared miraculously. But that was only one half of her life — there was the other half, her children, good Lord, yes. She glanced at the clock, one minute to two, and she could hear them already. She snatched a comb, combed her hair into a brave gray cloud over her head, and ran down the stairs.

'I wonder if it is the rodents or the equilateral triangle or the past participle this afternoon,' Clairette thought to herself with something like a sigh. How very differently life turned out to what one expected. Who would have thought when she and Doro and Annette first met that they would some day live in a little house together and teach school? Clairette hated teaching, especially the sort of teaching she was doing now, tutoring the hopeless children who couldn't pass their examinations, patiently repeating things over and over again, trying to extract a spark of intelligence. Clairette had never been born to teach, like Doro. It was not an adventure but a daily drudgery which she had to force herself by prayer to accomplish with any serenity. But when one imagined old age as a child it was always as a peaceful green island, the end of struggle and revolt, like the luminous end of the day. And here she was, still just as luxury-loving, just as wanting to be loved and just as tormented by continual revolt as when she was a little girl and had to learn her Latin grammar before she was allowed to have a blue ribbon for her hair. But she had come a long way. At least now she could laugh at herself a little, and at that exuberance which had led her to believe that life was a present wrapped up and delivered especially to her.

She had wanted fame. She had wanted glory. She had been muse to a whole group of French poets. At twenty she had been Spring, offering her first book of short stories like a bunch of forget-me-nots, so that one of them wrote: 'What dreams have you not dreamed? Who ever has been as young as you?' Love sprang up wherever she walked, as if she held a divining rod in her hand to tap the secret sources. She remembered days when she had felt so full of sweetness that it overflowed, when she used to have to run down the street so people wouldn't see that she was smiling. She had demanded happiness. She had accepted it as her right, and then she had had to renounce it, renounce it little by little, one happiness after another. It had given her face a gravity, a severity that lay like a mask upon it.

Clairette started as there was a knock at the door. She had been sitting with her chin on one hand at her desk for half an hour, and her arm was stiff.

'Come in!' There he stood, the little ogre, the fat little Deprès boy whom she hated and loved because she hated him, and because he seemed so little susceptible to her charm and she felt piqued.

'Oh, hello, André. What have you been doing with yourself all day?'

'Good morning, Madame,' he said with his back to her, struggling out of his coat. But he didn't answer her question. He was taking his copy books deliberately out of his satchel one by one, and apparently as slowly as he could. In spite of all her good faith Claire felt a dark rage welling up inside her. Why did she have to teach this grubby little boy his grammar? Why didn't he study better? Why was she so poor?

'Come and sit down, André. We have got to get the use of the past participle straight in our heads,' she said cheerfully and firmly, as if picking up her skirts to cross a puddle. Yes, the puddle had to be crossed, she thought to herself, looking very severe, the circles darker than usual round her eyes.

André sighed deeply.

'Come on, André. It's not as bad as that.' But the page in front of them looked very forbidding. 'What would you like to be when you grow up, André?' she said suddenly. If only he would say a painter or a poet they might reach some sort of understanding, the past participle would not need to be quite so divorced from them both, lying there on the cold page like a maze. André shot her a quick glance from under his eyelids, a suspicious and unrelenting glance.

'I don't know,' he said obstinately. And then Clairette, with her swift intuition, with her warm charm suddenly flowering in her hands, told him a story (forgetting entirely about the participles) about how she had tried to run away and join a circus when she was a little girl, how desperately she had wanted to be the girl in the pink satin tights who rode around the ring on a white horse standing on her head.

'I don't want to be that,' he said condescendingly. 'I want to be a clown,' he said, blushing up to the roots of his hair and looking down. Claire stared in astonishment at the impassive round face and the heavy eyelids. 'Oh, André, do you?' (How charming of him!) 'The last time I went to the circus was in Paris to see the Fratellinis. Have you ever seen the Fratellinis?'

'No, but I saw Poum once, only mother says I was too small to remember. He had a dog.' He looked away in this anguish of trying to recapture something he would never see again and couldn't remember really well enough.

'Poum was wonderful. I saw him twice, years ago. He did have a little dog, do you remember? A black dog with such a nice face who danced in a paper ruff.'

'His name was Cavalliera,' said André solemnly. 'He could count.'

'I wonder if I haven't a picture of them hidden away somewhere. Oh, André, do you think you could possibly learn this page while I am looking for the picture?' She looked at him pleadingly, and she was asking a courtesy now; she, a woman, was asking him to do her a favor. No man could have resisted those anxious blue eyes.

'I think I could,' he said gallantly. Claire patted his shoulder. She could have kissed him. She could have sung a loud song. Then she went into her bedroom, where somewhere there must be a bundle of old programs. Somewhere, somewhere there must be a photograph of Poum — or had she given it away? It would be terrible not to find it now. She knew that she was in grave peril as she took down a dusty package wrapped in brown paper and tied with blue ribbon. There they all were — Eve Lavallière in 'La Lettre Fatale,' Sarah Bernhardt with a palm leaf in her hand

— and a whole sheaf of the Experimental Theatre in Brussels — There it was! Cirque Royale. She could see the circular stage surrounded with boxes, the red velvet curtains, the sawdust ring in the centre, and the plush walls. There he was, Poum with his anxious face, the mocking eyebrows and huge sad mouth — There he was, and there was his little dog, Cavalliera. Oh, she could understand people giving up their family and friends, leaving their father and mother, giving up their wealth to join a circus.

'I've found it, André. I've found it!' She said, 'Look!' Now he would not have to try to remember any more. Poum was there. André's impassive face suddenly glowed, suddenly became transparent with joy. And after that they settled down with Poum in front of them to do something about the present and the past participles, though hard as he had tried, André had not done much toward cramming down the ten unreasonable rules.

'Well, here we are again,' said Claire, smiling over at him because she had won, because even now with her white hair and in spite of herself she had won. André was hers; this child accepted and adored her as all the others had done, as it was her right to be adored. He was incredibly stupid, she admitted with a smile, but he was really a dear. It would be nice if he could be a clown. It would be so much nicer than having him grow up to become head of his father's bank.

But still she had won. These were the things, the open human heart, this was the thing that could make her weep with joy and praise God and see the reason of the Scripture and believe in the immaculate conception.

More than a dogma, more than the wafer and wine of communion, this simple victory of the heart could fill her with the old tenderness for life, could make her overflow with sweetness, though André only looked at her with eyes full of undying devotion and still knew nothing about the past or present participle. Still, this was living, and now she knew that she could teach him a great deal.

Chapter Five

MARTHE looked at the clock once more and got up from her shining circle of pots to get the tray ready for Mamzelle Dorothée's tea. She was expecting company, it seemed, and would have it upstairs today: she had said: 'You had better bring it at four, Marthe. I have an idea that will be the zero hour today.' It was a shame that she was not coming downstairs to have tea with Madame and Mamzelle Anne: there were strawberries. It was a shame, Marthe thought, that Mamzelle had so little peace. There was always someone coming, and they all tired her out, she could see. Marthe would have liked to shut her demoiselles up as if this gay pink house were a convent — and she was quite right, for that is what they themselves would have liked best. Absorbed in these thoughts she had forgotten all about the handsome man sitting under the cross. There was the bell! Marthe wiped her hands hastily on her blue apron and went to the door.

'Is Mademoiselle Latour in? It is Madame Sauer. She is expecting me.' She was an attractive, well-dressed young woman, with a manuscript under her arm. Yes, they all brought manuscripts, every one of them.

'Yes, you can go right up,' said Marthe without

cordiality, showing her the way. Somehow or other they all found their way to the pink house, the young ladies who wanted to write; who wanted to write, most of them, because they were unhappily married, because at thirty they became terrified at the emptiness of their lives and found in Doro's blue room a sense of peace, of security, and more than anything a sense of a secret difficult adventure, which was living.

In the first half hour it all poured out, all the weight of their hearts. It was terrifying, Doro thought, how few people were happy — abysses lay all around one — and it was worth giving time and, more precious than time, the strength of the spirit, the little flood in the heart that might have made a poem, to help a little. In all the years that she had watched the unhappy young come and go, only twice had there been one of real talent — and then of course it made up for everything. There was Mélanie, now a dear friend, whom she had helped to write her first stories and who was now supporting her family. And there was Madeleine, the sculptress whom she had known as a child in the school, and who came to her one day with her arms full of flowers and burst into tears.

And now here was Eléonore Sauer, whose mother she had taught, intelligent, worldly. What did she want?

Marthe hurried down the stairs to ring the bell for the other two. They would be parched for their tea, she guessed, and this was Mamzelle Claire's day with André. Marthe was astonished as she looked out of the window on the landing to see that Madame was walking down to the garden gate hand in hand with that horrid little boy. 'They are all too good,' she thought jealously. 'They wear themselves out,' she thought. 'And then what happens? They are too tired to enjoy their suppers.' It was a shame.

Meanwhile downstairs Annette was covering a large round piece of bread with a thick layer of strawberry jam. Clairette came in from the garden door, pink in her cheeks.

'Clairette, you look as fresh as a daisy. What have you been doing with yourself?'

'Teaching André the participles, which I have an idea he will never learn in this world!'

Annette snorted through a large mouthful of jam and tea. 'I should think not. One might as well roar at a stone.' Clairette could very well imagine his impassive heavy-lidded face among the other children whom Didi could make laugh and cry at will, who were malleable and obviously learning something, Didi would say, were wide-awake, had feelings at least. But Clairette would never tell that he wanted to be a clown, nor that she had made a conquest of André and henceforth would champion him — *noblesse oblige*. 'I think he has a funny sort of charm, you know.'

'Piffle!' said Annette. She was fond of these archaic exclamations, and they suited her. 'What a sentimentalist you are. I suppose you will say in a minute that you feel sorry for him!' As that was just exactly what Clairette was about to say, she changed the subject quickly.

'Where is Doro?'

'Upstairs with Madame Sauer.'

'Oh.' It was not that they were jealous of these

people who came to see Doro, but they were jealous of her energy. They wanted her to themselves. They considered her their right, and tea seemed rather dull without her. The truth is that they had adapted themselves to each other so completely that when one was absent it was just like a trio without a violin. Nothing quite came off.

Clairette looked anxiously out of the window. The days were still so short. It was almost dark already. 'Pascal has forgotten his milk. I do hope nothing has happened to him.'

'He's probably hunting,' said Anne, reaching across the table for the hot water. 'Man does not live by bread alone. He lives by tea. I think I must have Irish blood, Clairette.'

'I shouldn't be surprised.' She had been looking out of the window into the mysterious dark world and the room reflected in it, but different, unreal as if they were under water having a mermaid tea. Now, turning to the actual world again, to the warm reality of objects, the teapot under the cosy, embroidered with a wreath (Doro had made it the year she was ill), looking at the blue cups and saucers and the yellow cream jug, shining every one of them, and then up at Annette's bright brown eyes, she said suddenly:

'My darling, I am going to get you a bright purple dress, and you must wear it. I *hate* that black dress,' she said savagely.

'Ma chère, I have never been a beauty, and long ago I decided that I preferred comfort. I like this dress because it has pockets, and I wouldn't care if it were yellow or red, for that matter; it is comfortable.'

'It is hideous,' said Claire relentlessly. 'You can have pockets in the purple dress I am going to give you, seven if you like, but it is not going to have a stiff collar!'

'All right, all right. Only leave me in peace.' What might have gone on for an hour — for they loved to play these passionate scenes, which usually ended in a physical battle and shouts of laughter — was interrupted by the arrival of Marthe to say, 'There is a gentleman in the hall.'

'Clairette, do you know who that is?' (The tone implied that it was a creditor coming to take away the furniture.) 'It is the prize-book man, and I haven't thought of a list yet. "Once more unto the breach, dear friends" — I suppose I shall have to see him. We can't afford leather bindings this year. They will have to be content with what is inside!' And she was gone. A door slammed. She was running upstairs. Every year there was this great affair of choosing the books to be given out as prizes at the last day of school.

Clairette was glad to be alone, not be be concerned, not to have to make any decisions. She went to the window and called: 'Pascal! Pascal! Come in, you rascal. Come and have your milk.' But there was no answer.

Annette thrived on war, on an atmosphere of haste and alarm. She loved to struggle with a mass of detail and emerge triumphant. She ran upstairs saying, 'George Sand, de Musset, René Boylesve — perhaps Shakespeare,' knocked on Doro's door, and burst in counting on her fingers 'George Sand, de Musset, Fabre.'

'Annette, what is the matter with you?' Doro sat up on her high bed, flushed and startled. She had been half asleep.

'The prize-book man is here and we haven't made the list!'

'I made a list last week,' said Doro quietly. 'It's there under the paper-weight on my desk. Come and read it over and see if you approve.' Annette brought it over and sat on the edge of the bed, too agitated to read it properly.

It was she who gave out the prizes every year. Doro really preferred to sit in a corner. She was desperately shy on these occasions, felt incapable of saying the right thing to the parents afterwards, wished always that she were invisible, could have written a secret message for each child in his book and then vanished. And Annette was wonderful with the parents. They came to her and talked at length about their children. She comforted them with her warmth and her sound common sense, with her humor and her perfect conviction that the children would learn in time.

'Well,' said Annette, swinging her legs, the bed was so high, 'I draw the line at Taine, but the rest looks all right. I must fly,' she said, jumping up without waiting for Doro's answer. 'I left the little man downstairs. Go to sleep again!' she called back. Doro thought she would go downstairs and have another cup of tea with Clairette. Eléonore Sauer had not stayed very long. She had left a pile of poems.

Clairette had been standing at the window with her nose pressed against it so as to be able to see the dark silhouette of the trees and the path instead of her own reflection. It was really very strange that Pascal hadn't come home yet. Could he have got run over? No, he was surely too clever and too sceptical for that. Perhaps he had gone to the neighbors, she thought with a pang. The pane was cold against her nose. The world looked very dark outside, grim. There was so little twilight these days. Night fell like a cloak. She shivered and turned away.

'Oh, Clairette, is there any hot water? Can I have a cup of tea?' Doro came in. She looked white, and Clairette was almost annoyed with her for looking so tired.

'I'm afraid it's lukewarm. Pour me a cup as well. You look tired, Doro.'

'Yes; it doesn't matter, though. Oh, how I long for a cup of tea!' She said, sinking into her chair and sniffing the tea as if it were opium: 'Tea is my vice, Clairette. Doesn't it always remind you of Liberty's in London? Like Aladdin's cave. We spent all our money and then went to that dreary ABC that we adored and drank strong tea and counted our pence to see if we could possibly get home on what was left.' And tea was opium to them both, the time when the past became a soft pleasant country of the imagination, lost its bitterness, ceased to devour, and in some tea-inspired way nourished them. They both sighed, as if for a moment the weight of living had slipped off their shoulders. They smiled at each other and drank their tea in little sips in silence, because as they were both thinking the same thoughts a word would have simply meant an interruption.

Doro was sitting in her usual chair, back to the great

door into the garden, but she turned quickly when she heard a thump on the window sill.

'Claire, there's Pascal.' There he was against the window, looking in. Clairette got up. Clairette went to the window with a little cry, for in his mouth was a white burden.

'Doro, Doro, he's caught something. It looks like a white pigeon. How horrible!' She opened the window. In walked the prince, his head held high in triumph, his mouth very wide open as if he were smiling, stretched to hold the white back.

'Is it dead?' At the marrow of their bones lay the ice of anguish.

'I think so. Oh, Doro, what shall we do?' They stood there looking at him in his triumph, helplessly.

'I'll try to catch him and you take the bird away from him,' said Doro in a frozen voice. In a second she had him by the scruff of the neck. 'Oh, poor little bird, poor little bird!' she said over and over, and then: 'Claire, it's one of the pouters from next door. How terrible!' she said, taking it tenderly in her hands as if this cherishing could alter death, change the world, as if by holding the warm soft body so gently in her hands something would be changed now, some peace might come to it.

'Oh, Doro,' she said in a soft voice of horror, 'the heart is still beating. Its eyes are open.' The bright fixed eye stared at them, 'the heart's beating, beating — oh, and he's bleeding,' she said as Doro passed him to her.

'Here, Pascal.' Doro picked him up by the nape of his neck. 'I'll put him in the kitchen and get a box so the poor thing can die in peace. We must leave it alone. We must let it die alone,' she said, running out.

The white pigeon never moved. It lay in Claire's hands, warm, with a single drop of blood on its back. Where was Doro? Why was she taking so long? Oh, God, she murmured, let it die quickly. The bright eye of anguish in the white head never wavered; the heart beat like a soft hammer inside.

At last Doro came back with a white wooden box lined with cotton. 'There, there, put him in, lay him there,' she said, wringing her hands, unable to be still, so helpless was she, and no heart could prevent this, no word, no gesture save. They must bear it.

'Come away, Clairette,' she said. 'We'll leave him here quietly. If only he could understand. If only we could explain that he can die now in peace.'

'At least they have no memory,' said Clairette. She laid him in the box and they tiptoed out and shut the door. They were both trembling now that there was nothing more to be done.

'We'll sit down a minute in the classroom before going up. It is terrible, terrible,' said Clairette. 'But he can't help it. It's his nature, after all,' she added, for perhaps the most painful part was not the white pigeon dying like a saint next door, but that Pascal, her cherished Pascal, had committed this crime. 'We shall have to tell the neighbors.'

'Yes.' They sat for a moment thinking of this. 'Come along, let's go upstairs. I felt quite faint,' said Doro, laughing.

At the top of the stairs they parted, Clairette pushing open her door and glad to be safe again in her own room.

She sat down at the desk with her head in her hands. It was quite still and peaceful.

But Doro felt shaken. She couldn't sit down but wandered from room to room, looking out of the window first at the garden designed black against the sky and somehow ravaged, she thought, as if aware of the crime that had just been committed there. She turned away, pausing for a moment before the drawing of Bird over the bookcase. Death — death. 'At least they have no memory,' Clairette had said, and she had meant the pigeon. But death, that was the terrible thing, death erased then the whole fabric of memory as well. Bird did not remember her now. She would not remember him. And for once the idea of the host of adorable dead, Shelley, Keats, de Musset, the great multitude who were there in the earth, did not comfort her. This was desolation. Doro sat at her desk with her head in her hands and tasted death.

Marthe had been told not to go into the dining-room, but that was half an hour ago and it was time to set the table. She wondered what she should do, looking at the clock and then apprehensively at the door as if one of her demoiselles might be standing behind it with her fingers on her lips like an accusing angel. Still, after all, they must have their suppers whether the white pigeon died or not. Pascal was sitting in the corner with his paws tucked in, looking fabulously pleased with himself. 'Pascal, you should be ashamed,' she said; but he wasn't listening at all, he was thinking long thoughts by himself, and only his tail acknowledged her presence by uncurling and giving a slow, irritated wag. 'Leave me alone. Let me dream in peace.'

Marthe crept out, closing the door softly behind her, ran across the hall, and paused a moment in the dining-room, listening. She thought she heard a whirring and then a thump. She opened the door a crack: 'Mary, mother of God!' she said, crossing herself rapidly. The bird had risen from the dead. He was sitting on the shelf by the window. She shut the door and fairly flew up the stairs to Mademoiselle Dorothée's door.

'Mamzelle! Mamzelle!'

'Come in, Marthe. What is it?' said Doro, thinking, I can't bear another calamity tonight, stiffening, though, to meet it, whatever it was.

'The bird, Mamzelle, the white pigeon — he's sitting on the shelf by the window. He's not dead at all. What shall I do, Mamzelle?'

'I'll come right down.'

As she opened the door Doro said: 'Don't be frightened. I'm going to let you out.' He was flying about the room, to the window and then back. She opened the window in a second, flung it open, and he was gone, gone out into the night, free, alive. Was this revelation? She had been wrong, then. One did perhaps rise from the dead.

As she went up the stairs to tell Clairette, Annette burst out of the schoolroom. 'Well, it's finally finished. He's the stupidest man we've ever had!' she ejaculated, coming up behind Doro and putting her arm around her. 'Why, Doro, you're trembling. What's the matter?'

'Come into Clairette's room and we'll tell you — the most awful thing! Pascal brought in one of the pouters from next door. We thought it was dying and left it there in the dining-room in peace. Half an hour later Marthe went in and it was flying about. Oh, Annie, I'm so glad!'

'I should think so. Pascal is a wretch — we shall have to tie a bell round his neck.'

Hearing this last Clairette came out of her room to say: 'Nothing of the kind: he would hang himself on that pointed fence. No, no.'

'The bird has flown away,' said Doro, embracing her. 'He is alive. It is all right, Clairette.'

So they all three went in and sat in Clairette's room under the lighted lamp, Annette with her stockings to mend, Clairette reading them her new story (she was writing the stories of the saints for her Bible class). — Doro sitting there silently, too happy and too tired to do anything but listen. It was the story of Saint Francis.

'Oh, my son most dear, how is it with thee?'

'By the grace of God, most well.'

By the grace of God, here they were, encircled with light, complete, with evening coming down and setting a seal on peace.

Chapter Six

IT SEEMED incredible to Doro, as she pushed open the door into her study after supper, that a day had slipped past, like a minute, like a year, or forty years, or a life. It seemed incredible, she thought, sitting on the corner of the sofa and looking out, that her entire life and all she had crossed of love, of sharpness and silence — a poor human thing, but a well where once or twice stars had fallen and once or twice an extraordinary cry tearing its blue — that all this could be summed up in a phrase like 'sixty-three years.' For sixty-three years she had been coming to this point, then. She had been coming to this moment at the end of the day to look out alone into a dark garden, at the outline of a cherry tree against the sky. And she said to herself, 'I am as gnarled, as rooted in the earth as that tree, as impersonal, as self-sufficient'; but even as she said it, putting her thought into a sentence and saying it as if that might fix it like a sign in the sky, even as she said it she knew that she lied. It was no use thinking she had arrived anywhere or was anything (but she must go to sleep now, and get up early in the morning to prepare the lesson on Claudel's 'L'Otage') — and it was no use imagining or saying that she was sixty-three years old when she was still so vulnerable, so expectant, so lonely, like a child wondering if she can get home in the dark before the wolf will devour her.

She got up and turned on the light, light that peopled the room, that gave her back the portrait of Bird with his kind eyes looking at her and the sketch of Pierrot in his big black hat — the two tiny paintings by Bird, the little golden swans, gold with the sun on them on a rainbow lake, and a tree in the Midi — brilliant, iridescent, more permanent, more brilliant than death or the dark. And the books! Light gave her back the books in their colored bindings. Light gave her back the past, nourished and warmed her with familiar things, unquestionable, there forever.

She would get undressed. She turned out the light and fled into the hall without looking back.

Getting dressed and getting undressed were the two most perilous moments of the day for Doro. When she was pulling her dress over her head and found herself in a shroud of material, panic took hold of her and she had to hold on to the basin to keep from falling. She could feel dizziness coming on like a shadow, like a tornado seen in the sky. She could always feel it coming on, and the trick was to manage somehow to get out of her dress and disentangled before it arrived. Then she could sit down and wait until it passed. Tonight she managed this very well, and got to the white chair just in time.

In her room Clairette was sitting in her blue wrapper on the flowered chintz cushions in the corner. This was her favorite moment of the day, a moment when austerity could be laid off like armor and she could sit in a soft silken wrapper with the smell of lavender and cigarette smoke about her, doing nothing. The curtains were drawn. On the desk in a neat white square lay her story, finished. She was thinking of the day, of the beggar-woman at church, of André, of Saint Francis, and then always in this moment of peace, of her dear, her beloved who must be somewhere not far away.

She questioned herself about her triumph with André, for she knew it to be a triumph, the old ardor welling up like a warm fountain inside her at the very thought. But she wondered if it were not once more an easy triumph, the triumph of personality, personality, she thought, that strange unknown quantity which was so inextricably of the flesh as well as of the mind and spirit. She had won, but she had won with old weapons; she had won with her heart and all that had made her a passionate imperious child, and not with the new stern pure fire she so greatly desired. Must this too be cut away? This simple outpouring, this use of an attraction that she could not explain but felt there in her finger tips like a divining rod, touching love wherever it lay, calling it out, saying, 'Here is the spring, here the source.' She had said as a young girl and it had become a sort of device: 'Don't smother your passion. Let it consume you. Let whatever must die in you die in the flame.' So she had loved Mentel with her whole being — and then he had died. Why? This was the question she asked herself over and over, the question that sent her back to seek a divine and not a human answer, that had made her hope to come at revelation through a ritual. And through the long prayers, the ceaseless setting of her questions beside the gold of absolute faith as one might set gilt beside gold, she believed she was finding a kind of peace.

Annette put on her woolen bed socks and sighed with pleasure at slipping into bed. With all the energy and violence of her actions of the day she now was still. She fell into sleep like a stone into deep water, untroubled, unresisting, with the pleasant always recurring image of the forests of the Ardennes where she had been a child coming and floating behind her eyelids just before she slipped off to sleep. She was practically invisible, as she always slept with the blankets pulled up over her head as if she were in a tent.

Doro wondered, as the dizzy spell passed, if she would call and ask Annette to help her undress and get into bed. She felt dreadfully weak, each garment an almost insurmountable obstacle between her and the safety of bed, every button a nightmarish puzzle that might bring on the whirling sucking sensation again. No, she would sit here another minute and then try once more. Annie would be fast asleep by now, dear Annie who would get up in a minute if she called. And between Clairette and her there was a shyness that forbade this sort of intimacy: only Annette was ever allowed to nurse her when she was humiliated by her body as she was now. She leaned her head against the back of the chair, turning toward it, setting the cool wood to sustain the pulsing forehead, to keep the fragile head from bursting apart in a thousand pieces. There, that was better. Keeping it there, she bent one hand down to take off her stockings and shoes, and in the same position to reach for her nightgown, pulling it off its hook.

Now she would rest for a minute. She felt so heavy it was difficult to lift her arm. So, little by little, with all the ruses she had learned through years of this, she managed to get undressed alone and creep along the corridor to her bed.

When her feet touched the hot-water bottle at the bottom a shiver went through her whole body like an electric shock, and then something like a sigh as she lay, afraid to move a muscle, feeling life come back into focus again and warmth slip through her feet to her spine. She would not sleep until the volcano, the multitude of nerves tense and erect, gradually loosened their grip and let her go. Always then she reached an extraordinary luminosity of vision. It was as if the tormented body turned the mind white-hot. Her life was clear before her as if seen from a great height, and now for the first time she had the impression that everything up to now had been a prelude, that she had been preparing herself for sixty-three years for something that must still come.

INNOCENT LANDSCAPE

PART II

Chapter One

AT NIGHT the town of Rye no longer seems like a spinster dressing up for a ball in her grandmother's dress. It loses its self-conscious air and becomes simply an old town in the dark, a still town where footsteps rattle like doom down the streets, and the stars one never sees in cities sit in the sky, a brilliant presence, so that one looks up instinctively instead of down. Mark shut the door behind him and considered the dark he was leaving: the panes glittering, the sense of something finished now he had left it, the self-sufficiency of this ageless house going back after the brief clatter of dishes and the rattle of coal in the scuttle, the occasional lamp and the narrow bed he had used — after this brief human interval the house perceptibly shut itself into some obscure timeless life of its own. He was rejected, forgotten as the starling whose nest he had burnt out of the chimney when he built the first fire there three months ago.

He picked up his bag and stood for a moment with it in his hand. The town itself all around him was still, the street lamp at the corner marking out the brass knockers, the locked doors, the blind windows. He glanced once up and down the street, up and down the three months past, and slipped one hand into his pocket as if there were some reassurance there, some link with what had just passed and what was to come. He put his hand in his pocket and looked up again at the sky. He set himself deliberately outside time, outside space in that second. He hated leaving. He hated pulling up from anywhere and leaving, but set yourself spinning in eternity for a second — it was an old trick — and the proportion changed. As he started forward he stumbled on the cobbles —

'Damn!' He had been adjusted to such vast spaces his feet had forgotten the small irregular path. Then he was off like a cat, for he had on sneakers. He left his bag at the station and came back through the town slowly, not looking up. He went up past the Oak House to the ledge where he could look over the marsh. Leaving, as usual, had made everything too clear and too sharp, made him feel as if he had had a shot of cocaine, like laughing and crying. Leaving was hell. It was true enough that the sky would be the same everywhere and the dark and the stars, and the earth the same under one's feet, and the same sort of people the world over. You could always find a friend, and the kind like Sam at the pub were the best, that asked nothing of you more than a smile and to be what you were; and the worst were like Al, that went off at a tangent into another world, dividing your mind and heart with talk of Communism or Pacifism, so that there was nothing in it but a cleft.

When Mark got to the sudden panorama, the immense marsh stretching out to the sea, he sat down on a bench with his head in his hands. He sat there and cursed because he was leaving this place where for some reason he had made roots, where he had written half a book, where he had sat in front of the fire one night and picked up that little yellow book. It had lain in a pile of odd things, a Spanish dictionary and some programs. One night he had been wandering about the house, restlessly picking up ash trays as if something might turn up under one of them, and then he had found this little French book: 'Poems, 1903,' signed Jean Latour. Never heard of him. He had sat cross-legged in front of the fire and picked up the book carelessly. He smiled, it seemed so old-fashioned and so French, and then he started saying some of it over to himself:

'The mournful village and my jealous heart.'

Still he could not admit that this Chopinesque poetry could mean anything to a man whose best friend had just joined the Communist Party. It was like dressing up, he thought, dressing up as a Watteau Gilles, but he went on reading. He pulled a pencil out of his pocket and began marking lines. He read it from beginning to end and felt as if he had discovered a drug that made the heart of man transparent — transparency, that's what it was. 1903, Jean Latour. He would be an old man now; he would be almost sixty, perhaps more. Mark got up and lit a cigarette. Still, it was worth the chance. It had been raining outside, thin, fine, persistent rain that would last for a day and a night. It was cold. He had got up and walked up and down, thrusting his hands into his pockets. Walking up and down, for once not listening, not maddened by the sound of his feet in the still house. 'I'll find him,' he said aloud.

(He remembered so clearly talking to himself.) 'One can't be born like that and change altogether.' Besides, he had been feeling restless for days. He must find a new place or a new person, or he couldn't work. He wanted the impersonality of travel again, the casual encounters, the feeling of being a ghost among men — and then he wanted to take a chance on Jean Latour.

Sitting on the bench he looked up and out at the plain, and the thin streak of light marking sky from earth at the horizon. It was as if he had found his direction like a compass: the needle pointed to Belgium, and it was time to go to the station for his train.

The doors were slamming, the thin owlish whistle hooting. Mark put his feet up on the old red cushion opposite, lighting a cigarette against the stale smell of beer and tobacco. The train was practically empty. Curious to be hurtling along through the dark in this prison. The excitement of the journey, of the beginning of the journey, was on him. He began considering what he would say to Morton tomorrow. He thought, with two months' work the poem should be finished — already he was leaping over it in his mind. He was thinking of what he should do next. But for the time being, with a pound in his pocket, yes, it was no joke. He would have to ask Morton for an advance, a humiliating business.

He thought of Al. He was sick of being alone. He wanted to be talking, drinking, sitting up all night laughing and forgetting to go to bed. Al, Al with his shock of yellow hair and funny clown face, Al driving an ambulance, fighting, believing fanatically in one way for the world. He could hear him saying: 'There's no time for thinking, Mark. It's a luxury and a waste these days. We've got to clean this mess up.' And Mark all the time feeling he must withdraw, think, be silent. In three months alone in that house he had had a curious feeling of growing transparency. He almost wondered if he would ever veer back again to the opacity, the necessary walls of social personality. It would be strange to see Carson and the old gang again. They would always be there, he thought. There would never be any cleavage with them — they didn't believe anything enough. And he preferred Al, though it was hard to admit something so imponderable, so strangely stern, had come between them. He knew that their lives were separated now forever, separated by an idea. Strange ——

He had been twenty when he met Al in a bistro in Paris. He remembered it clearly, the big baggy-looking boy with narrow blue eyes darting at you and then away, so full of vitality it was like standing against a wind. He was telling a story about Ireland — all Al's stories were about Ireland, with a vocabulary full of stiff gold words and Lawrence of Arabia, a sense of the march of sentences. When the story was finished Mark said in English, 'Come and have a brandy.' He said it although he didn't have the money to pay for it. It was nine o'clock. They had talked all night, and then Al had said, 'Come and live at my place until you get your bearings.' He worked in a travel office. This was the sort of thing that always happened to Mark. He felt sometimes he must be lucky, such strange necessary things happened to him always. Now, this

Jean Latour — this Jean Latour — but the wheels were scraping. The thin owlish whistle was hooting. He would have to change at Ashford. He jerked himself back across the Channel, across time, across England. He buttoned up his trench coat and opened the window. The moon was setting already, the sky gray and black and torn across with orange light. They were screeching, scraping into Ashford.

Then another train, another setting out, another train of thought, changing trains, changing tracks, and all bound through this night for Belgium, for a little dark country where he had heard one ate well. Strange, strange life — stranger, he said to himself. This was the sort of thing words did, slipped one into another, said 'stranger' after saying 'strange.' Already he was a stranger to this country and this people who ate vegetable marrow. He was falling asleep.

The express from Ashford to London rocked from side to side with a monotonous irregular motion like a mechanical gallop. Mark, alone in his compartment, was lying full length on the red seat with his trench coat over him and a blue sweater under his head. He was lying on his back with his arms crossed tightly under his head. Asleep, his face looked old and worn, worn from the inside as if something had been stretched too far and might break. He might have been a soldier coming back from the front — it had that look of tenseness, of a mask worn uneasily from necessity. He frowned and murmured, 'Jean Latour,' then jumped up and swung his feet down. His own voice had woken him. There was no one in the compartment. He yawned and lay down again with his face to the wall. Another half hour before Victoria.

Chapter Two

MARK rang Carter's bell, the top floor of an old house in Bloomsbury. He'd sent a post card the day before. Carter must be expecting him and might have a bed.

'Hello!' His brisk editorial voice: 'Come on up!'

There were three of them, drinking tea on the floor in front of a gas fire. 'Come and join the fray — how's the book?' Carter always made him uncomfortable with his professional literary manner: he ran a small poetry magazine. The other two Mark didn't know. He never listened to names when he was introduced.

'Hey, hold on. Do you want four lumps?' Once Mark was settled, he looked around. Beside him on a cushion was a dark square-faced boy, looking vaguely familiar.

'I've seen you somewhere, of course, but God knows where.'

'He acts,' supplied someone very young with a tow head and a ferret face in the corner.

'Oh.' Mark could find nothing else to say. He was embarrassed at their attention; the three heads were all watching him stirring his tea with a spoon — their conversation interrupted, an unknown quantity projected into their atmosphere, the current stemmed by his entrance; and now he was holding everything up like a twig in a stream, collecting the impact of their thoughts as they gathered one by one. Mark went on stirring his tea.

'You know, Mark' — it was Carter, sitting cross-legged, belligerent, ready for action, for conversation, for excitement — 'you are fast becoming a legend in England.' For some reason the incongruity of the last three months, now that he was back here, with the usual our-little-circle-superiority going on, swept over him. Which was real? Which was himself? His mind galloped along in a train to Belgium, but here he was sitting in front of the fire, laughing.

'God, Carter, you ass! My book has sold three hundred copies — what are you talking about? I wish I were one of these chaps who could fit their time so comfortably and say what needs to be said.' Now that he was started off he was delighted to have an audience of three, no one to talk to for three months. Suddenly the desire to talk, to make a noise, to be heard, took hold of him violently. 'But I think it's a good thing. It may be dangerous to be too mixed up with ideas of destiny, the world to be changed — or even new ways of speech. "Who remembers the address of the Imagists?"' he added, and drank his tea down at a gulp.

The ferret-faced boy lit a cigarette. 'I envy the chaps who can clear out and risk their lives getting potatoes to Spain — something definite like that.' He was rocking with his toes in his hands. Mark thought, he looks like a weasel, but it is pleasant rather than unpleasant. He said:

'What keeps you from going? It's a cause, if that's what you're looking for.' But what made Al pack up for Spain while he shut himself in an old house to write a long poem in Spenserian stanzas? What made one thing possible and another not? He would throw himself into a river without thinking to save a man — why couldn't one conceive in terms of the many?

The ferret-faced boy was rocking back and forth chewing his cigarette. 'Because I don't believe in it enough, for one thing.' He looked like a nice weasel, Mark thought.

'I'm so sick of this sort of conversation; silly, useless' — the actor trying so hard not to look like an actor that he was unmistakeable, the open flannel shirt, the consciously worn tweeds. Strange breed they were, strange to use yourself as a medium. Mark laid his teacup down and settled back out of the light. He was bored. Silly, useless, yes, conversations like this between people, no exchange, really ——

'In the theatre,' the actor was happily beginning, was expanding, 'we escape it less than anywhere else. We *must* lead or perhaps guess at the subconscious desires of the masses before they know themselves what they want — give them what they hope, what they have not quite dared to hope. And yet how boring the prophetic individual can be. Gordon Craig — my God! — sitting over his sets like a huge inescapable ego — the arrogance of it. And yet,' he added, turning to Mark, 'it's so boring, these social plays, these earnest schoolmarmish appeals — it's all so raw, isn't it?' He turned to Mark, who had not been listening but was watching him, wondering what he was like underneath. He sounded as if he had heard all this before, said somewhere else, and repeated it, somehow losing the point in the process. He turned to Mark and added, 'Why don't you write a play?'

'Nice and incisive, with a bit of satire in it' — Carter leapt at the chance. He liked important moments to take place in his rooms. He could say afterwards, 'Oh, yes, we persuaded Mark to write that play one night last year.' He was standing up.

'Write a play about Matteotti.' He threw his cigarette into the fire.

'It could be marvelous!' It was the ferret-faced boy. They were all after him, full of ideas, bursting with energy, and he had nothing to say, nothing to do but go and talk to some lyric old man in Belgium. Mark felt tired as hell. Oh, leave me alone, he wanted to say. I know I'm no good. I'll never do what you want, what ought to be done.

'A play about Matteotti.' He threw his cigarette into the fire with all the impatience one hand and a little object and the distance of a yard to the grate could express together. He flung his cigarette into the fire, flung it away with their easy significant ideas. 'A play about Matteotti — yes, it could be good,' he said. 'But I couldn't write it,' he added bitterly. Bitterness filled the room, became, like everything Mark did, curiously theatrical, imposed itself on the others.

They sat silent, not looking at each other, thinking of bed, of sleep, of getting a drink at the corner. They sat each apart wishing he were alone.

But Carter would not let them be alone. Kindly, persuasively he must bring them back, pit them against each other, bull and matador, if there was to be any conversation.

'You've been away too long, Mark. It's dangerous to stay away so long. Besides, we need you here.'

'Like hell you do!' Mark laughed. He wished it were true. He was envious of the two or three men of his kind, men whose business was words, who were really needed — or thought they were. 'Well, give me the cause and I'll die for it. But I'll never write for it.'

'"It is the cause, it is the cause, my soul."'

'Oh, shut up, John, for Christ's sake.' They laughed at him, murmuring words another man had written, Mark thought, making himself a mirror for another man's mind; but he liked him. He was not stupid, after all. They were all in the same boat really, he thought.

'Shipwrecked in the twentieth century' — it was the ferret-faced boy picking up Mark's thought as if it were there, a card on the table.

'Rot!' Carter pulled his vermilion tie tight. 'You think you're so damned exceptional. What about a man like Herrick? He was in just the same dilemma' (Carter liked words like dilemma. He bit off their tails as he spoke them) 'but he went on cosily writing lyrics to Julia. God knows why everyone has suddenly developed a supersensitive conscience toward the race at large.'

'A sort of horrid change of life in mankind itself.' The ferret-faced boy had edged nearer to Mark. The room was smoky, dank. Mark felt tired, and this human creature edging nearer made him nervous. Probably imagination. He hadn't seen his own kind —

if these were his own kind — for so long, he'd forgotten how people behaved. Still, the invisible antennae of the body were standing erect. He got up.

'I've got to see my publisher tomorrow early, catch him while he's fresh. I think I'll turn in. Carter, have you a bed for me?'

'Don't go yet.' The ferret-faced boy yawned and stretched. 'How can you bring yourself to move? How can you go over there in the cold?' He was hugging his knees and rocking back and forth again.

Mark stood at the window with his back to the room. There wasn't a soul in the street, just the regular pattern of the street lamps, the red glow of the sky overhead. It might have been the eighteenth century. Carter was saying;

'Yes, come along. I'm afraid it won't be very comfortable.'

They were all getting up, getting into coats and mufflers. The room, which had been held fixed around their four selves, suddenly disintegrated into the stains on the armchairs, the newspapers left untidily in a corner, the separate books — and they themselves were reduced to a green muffler the actor was tying too carelessly round his throat, and the ferret-faced boy's moist hand shaking Mark's:

'Good night. Come and see me sometime. I have quite a nice flat, just three or four blocks away — Taviton Street.'

'I'm going to Belgium'; and as Mark said it, it was as if someone had said, 'Africa — Italy,' and in some play he had seen, 'Wien! Wien!' as the curtain came down. 'I am going to Belgium' meant all the pomp and ache of cymbals, the shiver of apprehension like love. He had forgotten about it entirely in the last hour, and now it was a dazzling thought. They all turned to him, the two at the door, and Carter, throwing ashes from an ash tray into the wastebasket, stopped.

'Well, it's cheap, anyway,' said Carter.

'And rather swell if you like scudding clouds, an ominous sky over ancient towns, that sort of thing,' the actor said with a question on the end (You don't really like that sort of thing, do you?).

'Well, we'll see. I don't know yet whether I shall like it or not' — though the sky and the earth would have very little importance if there were someone to talk to. 'Good night, glad to have met you,' he said warmly; but the warmth was not for them but the joy that welled up inside him like a fountain. He went out to the landing with Carter and waved to them at the bottom. Then the door slammed.

'I'll tell you about it in the morning, Carter.' Carter was a good friend after all. There was always a bed here, and the sense of one's own importance seeped down from the ceiling and up from the blankets. You were surrounded and bolstered up by others like you, the world diminished to a set of emotions and possibilities held within this strict circle. You were one thing or another. You were not, had nothing to do with a man called Jean Latour.

Mark couldn't help smiling at Carter's certain scorn if he were to come across a tiny yellow book printed in 1903 saying nothing except the peace of two people and their sole adventure. But there was 'Verse and Prose' confidently asserting that writing these days could only be one thing — to live. Use this phrase, this particular combination of sentiment and political convictions, and your soul would be saved in the next world. And the awful thing is, thought Mark, turning out the light and stretching flat on his back, the awful thing is that I almost believe it myself. I almost believe — but he was too sleepy to finish. And there were the publishers tomorrow, green doors to be faced, secretaries, the inevitable sense that they were doing him a great favor to publish him at all. He jumped out of bed to open the window. It was warm outside, warm and spring, the country of the night: Belgium was there somewhere, miles away in the dark.

Chapter Three

MARK took a clean shirt out of his bag. The breakfast tray was full of cigarette butts. It looked cold and gray out. A man was trying to sell ice cream on the corner to people in macks hurrying along. Well, he must be off. Half-past nine — there was time to walk there; walking would keep him busy, keep him from thinking too much. Curious, these conscious snares of the mind, the mind living in constant fear of the unknown, the terrified, the sudden creature below who might rise up at any moment and say, 'I'm not going.'

He turned down a wide empty street flanked with Georgian houses, cool, impersonal — he felt his presence drawing the scene to a perspective as if he were an actor on a stage and the street painted on a backdrop. He felt the sharp point of himself giving this cold street meaning and proportion, giving it life. Life, life, life, his feet drummed out on the pavement; a taxi, turning the corner clumsily, gave a hoot of derision.

Somewhere in the next street a piano on wheels was playing 'Alone — ta, da, dadadada-daa.' A messenger boy on a bicycle went by whistling. Mark dropped a penny in a hat on the pavement in front of a chalk drawing of the Union Jack with 'Good luck' on it; he did it for luck, not looking at the man squatting somewhere behind it on no legs. He couldn't stand looking into beggars' faces. It made him uncomfortable, made him each time examine his own conscience, go through a dialogue with himself: 'Why don't you do more with your time, with your three meals a day and your comfortable bed, with your Oxford education?' For some reason he always said that sentence like a Salvation Army tune whenever he was confronted with a beggar, and it was sillier and more unreal because he had never been to Oxford, never been properly educated at all; but still that was the inevitable sentence his conscience turned on, which he had to listen to — and though it was so unreal, had somehow to try to answer.

How much had he worked? Of what was he deserving that he was walking so quickly down Gordon Square with his feet beating out 'Life, life, life' on the pavement? This was not the moment to ask himself such a question. Better to buy the violets, Parma violets in a great basket on the corner. But what would he do with a bunch of violets? He thought of Jean Latour buying them in Ghent as he must have done for one of his frail girls in their white dresses. But to whom would he send violets? When he imagined a girl, the sort of girl you would send violets to, she had no sort of reality, no breasts, and legs where the thin evening dress showed the aristocratic bone: she was rather like the cherubim at the bottom of the Sistine Madonna. She was not real at all. She was something to fill in the awful moment between his first sight of the building and his pushing open the green door and saying to the secretary (who was not one to send violets to):

'I have an appointment with Mr. Morton at ten.'

'Your name, please?' She didn't look up.

'Mark Taylor.'

'You may go right up.'

Morton's room was big and messy, with two enormous desks covered with magazines and books and papers. Morton, behind this barrage, sat in a swivel chair puffing at his pipe — genial, blue-eyed, middle-aged. Mark shook hands with him across the desk.

'Well, it's nice of you to come in and call on us, Mark.' He was shuffling about among some papers. 'Seen this?' He was always bringing out prizes (the gesture, a prize-giving gesture). He gave Mark a red-covered book.

'No.'

'We're quite pleased about it — like to know what you think of it.' He sat back in his chair watching Mark open the book and glance inside.

'Where have you been all this time? And how's the book?'

'I don't know. I like it, but I doubt if anyone else will.'

'We're anxious to see it, you know. When do you think I could have a glance at it?'

'Well' — this was what he had been waiting for — 'I think I can hand it in finished in two months.' Mark was sitting forward, looking down. He must come to the point. He must concentrate himself, not let the creature, the savage creature inside him, make him lower his eyes. This was fatal.

'I want to go to Belgium to finish it. I have a reason for going there. I wonder,' he said clearly and loudly —

he realized that his voice was pitched high and felt like a schoolboy — 'I wonder' (Morton was leaning forward playing with a pencil) — 'I wonder,' he began again, looking out of the window, 'if you could give me something to live on until I can finish it.'

Morton slid easily back into his chair with the pencil held in his two hands, then he let it fall on the green blotter and knocked his pipe against the side of the desk. Each of these small movements accomplished quickly and easily took on for Mark the exactitude, the portent of a slow motion picture of a prize fight. They seemed interminable. It was possible that Morton would never speak at all, that words were something his mind had invented in a moment of madness. Perhaps this tapping of a pipe on a desk was the only human method of communication. Mark was staring straight at Morton. He felt like an animal who tries to speak and can't.

'I wish I could.' There, it was all over. No hope, finished. Mark fished in his pockets for a cigarette. His hand was shaking. 'You see, Mark, we do believe in your stuff and in its eventually finding a public. But unfortunately — or fortunately, perhaps, for you — you are not fashionable. You are not, just now, the thing. You are, in fact, rather a luxury to a publisher.' Mark was hardly listening; all this he had said to himself so often that it might have been a speech from a play. But the voice was going on: 'Why don't you write a novel, Mark?' Well, why shouldn't he? It was simply beyond his imagination, the sheer labor, the immense bulk of it.

'But Mr. Morton' — now that it was all over he could talk — 'I want to finish this book. I suppose a long, sustained poem like this is something like a novel. There's a stream going on underneath all the time. I wouldn't dare stop now, even if I could write a novel the way one brings a rabbit out of a hat —— Good God, I've lived for the past three months on a pound a week. That's all I ask.'

Morton was filling his pipe again. For some reason he reminded Mark of the caterpillar in Alice. It was a burden, he thought bitterly, to have a mind that converted every damn thing into something else.

'You'd need about ten pounds. You could do it on that, you think?'

'Yes.'

'How about doing some criticism? Theatre? You've always had ideas about the theatre.'

'But I have to go to Belgium.'

'Oh, yes, I'd forgotten about that.' Morton looked at him out of the corner of his eye. 'What's taking you to Belgium, Mark? Not a girl?' Not a girl. Mark laid the red book on the desk.

'No, not a girl.' He got up and stood a minute with his hand on it. 'No, not a girl,' he said, smiling.

'I have an idea. Do an article — "My Contemporaries" — as hard-hitting as you like. Bring it in next week.' Next week — next week was too far away, with a mountain to cross before he would reach the end. 'Do an article.'

'How many words?'

'Not more than five thousand.'

'All right. I'll try. Thank you, Mr. Morton. I'll come in next week.'

'Until then, do you want me to lend you a pound?' Here it was again, the nettle in the bed.

'Thanks. I'll be all right until then.' Get out. Run away. 'Cheerio,' he said loudly, wondering if Morton saw the blush that was flooding up under his collar. He ran down the stairs and out. Here at least in the street no one would notice him. He could be anonymous for a little while. He walked toward the Russell Hotel. From a distance it looked like an absurd castle, the sort of edifice which is named 'So-and-so's Folly'; there was a flag on each turret. It looked, he thought, like an illustration for the Green Fairy Book he used to read as a child. It was not real. He walked quickly past the doorman and up the absurd red-carpeted staircase. Here he would meet no one. He had never stepped inside it before. He walked into the reading-room, with its black leather armchairs and smell of tobacco and magazines. 'See England by car' — 'Air-France.' He sat down with a pile of folders and lit a cigarette. Camouflage. No one would speak here, no one would look at him, no one he had seen before or ever would again.

But even here he must be someone, he must be himself, he must listen to himself saying, 'Five thousand words, you fool. Anyone could do that.' Looking at a drawing of the newest air liner with private bathroom, his indefatigable mind was saying, 'Go home and get to work.'

Between action and action there are bridges and abysses to be crossed, and sometimes there is no bridge and one has to try to find a way to leap over. As Mark sat looking at the newest monoplane: 'For the price of a Ford car you can have wings,' he was hunting for a place to jump over. It was too easy to live alone and work quietly at a poem for a month. It was too damned easy to say, 'Only my work is important'; to say, 'I'll get Morton to give me an advance'; to say, 'I must go to Belgium to find Jean Latour,' when the answer was 'Get to work and write a five-thousand-word article and you will jump over from action to action.' It looked easy, but he felt sick, sick with himself and his soft too aware mind that understood itself so completely and found excuses for itself.

Opposite him as he flicked an ash off his cigarette his eyes met another pair of eyes, a shrewd pair of eyes that had been watching him, he felt sure, watching his hand flick over the pages of 'Air-France.' He wondered for a second if by any chance he had been talking aloud. Even from here he was being driven out. He was being found out. He was meeting challenge. Even here in this anonymous, almost totally anonymous, room one did not escape the eye of consciousness. He slammed down the magazine and walked out.

Food. He would eat. For the price of a Ford car you can have wings. For the price of a ham sandwich you can manage to live. He went into a little place and ordered coffee and a sandwich. Just opposite him in the corner was a telephone booth. It occurred to him that he might call up someone. He might say: 'Come on. Let's go out and get drunk.'

But Belgium lay somewhere beyond this moment. He could only reach it by jumping over, by finding a way across. Jean Latour could not be the means but the end. Something had to be accomplished, like the prince in the fairy tale before the reward. And dragons everywhere. Now there were two things (one hand in his pocket felt for the single shilling). There were two things possible. (He laid the shilling absent-mindedly on the counter and looked at it there, but there was no change. It was taken away and nothing given him in return.) Two things: one, to ring up the ferret-faced boy, get drunk, maybe borrow the money — or Mrs. Barrett, who would give him tea, who would ask him what was wrong and say, 'But of course, my dear boy. Why make such a fuss about it?' The other, to go back to Carter's flat and write the article.

There is, for instance, time. These matters take place in the flash of an eye, in the instant it takes the pupil to enlarge as it looks into the eye of love, as the lights go out. In this flash of a second the shutter of the soul snaps, the photograph of action is taken. And so every action by the time it happens has already been recorded. It is the past. The present is the past already.

When the shilling clicked on the desk and the door slammed shut behind him, something had happened that was as loud as trumpeting.

Chapter Four

CARTER came in at five o'clock and found Mark asleep on his bed. The typewriter held a sheet in it, and there was a pile of papers beside it. He smiled. Mark had evidently been working. Mark had been working in his flat, and he thought of it with satisfaction. He whistled a little Glück as he went to the kitchen to have a drink.

'Hello, Carter' — Mark turned over and stretched — 'Give me a drink like a good chap.' Something had happened. Some great event had taken place. 'Oh, yes. I have written an article.'

'What article?'

'Oh, an article for Morton. It's finished. It's done. Hurrah!' he said, getting up. 'Carter, I'm beginning a new life. Something has happened at last. At last something of importance has taken place in your rooms!'

'Well, well! Let's have a drink on it.' Carter's imperturbable geniality enveloped him like an eider-down.

'But Carter, in order to begin this new life I must have some dinner. I spent my last shilling five hours ago. I'm starving.'

'Here, drink this. We'll go out and eat.' Mark's

hand shook as he took the glass. He noticed it and was amused. It shook, he supposed, because he had been writing steadily for hours, but it looked absurd. Now that the thing was done, it was hard to remember the extravagance of the last hours. He felt ashamed of himself. From now on he would live like other people. He would earn his living. He would wear a tie and a waistcoat and read the papers and form opinions. He would write serious essays.

'How about the Café Royale? I feel garrulous. I feel like talking noisily and making rude remarks about people.'

'Right. Let's go.'

Carter was a good companion. He never impinged, but flowed comfortably along beside one. He was eternally and always perfectly adapted to a situation, and just sufficiently conceited so that he never became absorbed. As they walked down the street Mark looked at him sideways.

'You know, Carter, you have a pretty good life.'

'Why does that occur to you just now?'

'I have a sudden respect for the bed and the breakfast and the work cut out for you. But do you ever get bored, Carter?'

But Carter was running for the bus. He would always be propelled into action at the moment when he might become bored. There was always the immediate outer necessity to take the place of any inner necessity. He would never be dissatisfied with where he was going, because he would not imagine any other possible route.

They were in the bus, sitting sideways, looking out at a stream of color, of people caught sight of and then lost, one after another, quick impressions glanced at involuntarily and faithfully recorded by the eye, by the mind. It should be possible to function or not, as one chose. The mind was like a horrible glutton who ate everything he saw. Mark shut his eyes. The lurching made him dizzy. But there were artificial methods of shutting it, blunting it, blurring the individual too-clear image, making the kaleidoscope with all its bright pieces merge into one soft color.

They were sitting at the table nearest the door, Carter and he, and two empty glasses, with the waiter setting down two clean ones and dexterously tipping the bottle of brandy to the desired place. This was one method of temporarily holding off the machinery of consciousness. Mark felt pleasantly dazed. Carter felt comfortable and amused. There were many people here that he knew by sight, by reputation. He felt pleasantly like God as the door opened to let in a man in a blue shirt.

'There's Pash. My God, his last stuff has fallen off. Did you see his show?'

'I used to like what he did.'

'Well, his color's gone off completely and he's trying to do landscapes, poor man. I met Lady B on the street, and she was hesitating whether to buy one and hurt his feelings by not hanging it, or not to buy one and hurt his feelings.'

'I used to like his work,' said Mark. He watched the man in the blue shirt stand looking for a table as all eyes turned to him, turned to any point of color or movement in the room, thinking he looked vaguely like

Saint Sebastian if eyes were arrows. Mark picked up his glass.

'Oh, there's Georgia,' Carter's voice went on comfortably. 'We must go over and speak to her.' Mark drank down the last of his second brandy. Why look at Georgia, whoever she was, be told that she drank too much or had had an abortion last year? He was thinking, brandy is one way of making the kaleidoscope still for a second. Love, he was thinking, love is another. Love ——

'Who's that, Carter?'

'I just told you — Georgia Manning. You know, paints psychoanalytic portraits.'

'Oh.' She was standing in the door waiting for somebody, half turned away from the room, hesitant. She had on a hat made of black feathers. It fitted her head like a cap, hiding her hair. It was the hat that made her look like a bird. Her shape was like a bird, the small aristocratic head, the long neck and the broad shoulders, hips, the awkward gait that made her now shift from one foot to the other. She was greeting someone just coming in, a middle-aged, thin, alert little man. They walked past arm in arm.

She looks like a swan, Mark thought. 'Who's that with her?'

'Oh, that's Manuele, her husband.'

'She's married?'

'Been married for years. She's not young, you know. Married Manuele, and a jolly good thing too. He's managed her ever since, made her, really. Nice little man. Have another brandy?'

'No, thanks. Yes—yes, I will.' (She looks like a swan.)

'Two again, please.'

(She looks like a swan, the curious erect carriage, the awkwardness, the grace. Georgia Manning — Georgia Manning — oh, yes, in Paris.) Now he remembered: 'I saw a landscape of hers in Paris once.'

'What are you mumbling about, Mark? She's never painted a landscape in her life.'

'No, no. I'm sure. I went back to see it twice.' They turned round to find out where she had gone. They turned together as they talked and watched her, watched Manuele pull a table out and them both sit down, watched her take off her gloves and open her coat.

'Would you like to meet her? I'll take you over.'

'No, no. Not yet. I'll finish my brandy.'

Things happen too quickly when they happen. There is never time to discover the reason, the way out, the sensible end. The article finished, the way to Belgium open. One sits in the Café Royale and a woman with a feather hat on who managed to paint a landscape you can't forget must walk in at just that moment. You are in the middle of a piece of work. You are writing quite calmly in the garden and a bird comes and does something on your head. Some people call that luck. Some people say it is the ultimate violation to have a bird do something on your head. Mark thought, Remember that you have had two brandies and are about to have a third. Keep that constantly in your mind, you fool, and forget that love is one of the things that can blur the horribly distinct images that keep dancing in front of your eyes.

'Well, shall we go?' (You have had two brandies.

It is equally possible to go out of that door on the left and tomorrow embark for Belgium. Tomorrow you will remember that you were drunk in the Café Royale and saw a woman with a feather hat on, and that will be all. You have had two brandies ——)

'I have had two brandies.'

'Three, Mark, if you must be exact. Come on.' They were getting up. This is how one feels when one is swimming under water. Through time, through everything that had happened to him up to now, Mark was swimming slowly and exactly. That is a table. That is a chair. You must go round and not over or through them. For a moment the room blurred and his feet alone found the way. Then in the immediate foreground before him was a face. It looked inquiringly as he heard his name;

'Georgia, this is Mark Taylor.'

'Sit down and have a r-r-r' — (it sounded like a purr) 'and have a round.' He thought rapidly, It is impossible to be a bird and a cat at the same time. She is not a bird. She is a cat in bird's clothing. He smiled, but it was at himself, not at Manuele, who was just then pulling out a chair for him and saying:

'Sit down. Sit down. We are feeling dreary. We are hating London.'

'We are feeling hungry.' Carter slipped easily into the groove made for him by Manuele. 'The trouble is that we have had no dinner. It has given Mark hallucinations. He says he saw a landscape of yours in Paris, and I told him you'd never painted a landscape in your life.'

'Oh, yes, I did.' When she talked she looked down

and smiled. Her eyes were half shut. 'I painted one landscape years ago. How strange that you should have seen it.' But she was not looking at him. She was leaning her elbows on the table and smoking. Her hands were broad like a man's, and she used them in strange ways, as if she were subconsciously observing them, as if they belonged to someone else in whom she was very much interested.

'It was in Paris. I went back twice to look at it, and then the exhibition closed. It's the only thing I have seen of yours.'

'Georgia is having an exhibition next week. You must come.' As Manuele spoke Mark turned to look at him. Green eyes, long delicate hands. He was quiet but nervy, watchful. So now he was watching Georgia finish her drink, and had signaled a waiter before she put it down.

'I shan't be here next week' (No, by God if I have any sense). 'I am going to Belgium.' But he had said it so many times before. He had heard himself say it so often in the last two weeks. 'To finish a book,' he added.

'For some reason Mark thinks he can finish his book in Belgium.'

'Oh, yes, I can understand that.' Manuele lit her cigarette as she spoke, and she was still looking away. 'It is a country that ignores one and never imp — ppinges.' He saw now that whenever she cared about what she was saying she said it to herself. The last words were inaudible. It sounded like 'I spent April there once,' but no one would ever know what it was she said.

'I am staring at you,' said Mark suddenly, 'I am being very rude.'

'Oh, one expects to be stared at in this place.' It was Carter slipping tactfully in, of course. 'Besides, Georgia is used to it.'

'You had better eat something, now it is here,' said Manuele quietly. The fact is, thought Mark, I am drunk and nothing of this is real. This horrible ache in my chest is just because I am drunk. It is not because she has not looked at me and I don't know the color of her eyes. It is not because that man with green eyes is her husband. It is because I am hungry and drunk. As he thought all this Mark picked up a fork and began to eat silently and savagely. While he ate he was aware that they were talking around him. Somewhere very high up above voices were talking lightly and airily. It was too difficult to distinguish the words, but it was fun to wait for Georgia to purr on an r, to hesitate in the middle of a word, to catch her breath. Now Manuele was saying:

'We must be going.'

'Yes, we must. I have a sitting at nine tomorrow morning.'

'We must,' said Mark suddenly, leaping into complete possession of all his faculties and addressing himself to Carter. 'I have to see Morton tomorrow. And besides, I couldn't bear ——' (I couldn't bear this place without Georgia Manning. It would be too empty, but quick, don't say that, think of something else.) He looked up and met her eyes as he said again, 'I couldn't bear ——' But the sentence was finished in another way.

'Come along, pussy.' Manuele helped her on with

her coat. As she came in, she went out, on his arm, slowly.

'She looks like a swan.'

'Well, that's that,' said Carter. 'Do you really want to go? How about some coffee?'

'No. I feel ill, Carter — I think we'd better go.'

'Right.'

They were in a taxi. By some miracle they had extricated themselves from the lights and the tables. They had found a door and a way out, and now they were in this pleasant, enclosed dark.

'You're not really drunk, Mark. It's impossible. You only had three brandies.'

'No, tired. I have hallucinations. Swans and things.' Sleep now. Forget it. See what a night can do. Wake up in the morning and get tickets for Belgium. Out of all anguish, out of this moment and out of all others in the last two weeks, Belgium and Jean Latour spelled peace. But tomorrow, just tomorrow he would telephone. He would ask if he could call. He would discover the color of her hair. Tomorrow he would telephone her. He would say, 'You have a hat with feathers and I have never seen your hair'; and he would say other things clearly.

Chapter Five

IN THE morning the things that flower in the seascape of the night close like sea anemones at the touch of a finger. Mark woke up to the grating of the curtains' being pulled back by Carter. He woke up to coffee and a boiled egg, to a pile of manuscript all out of order to correct and rewrite. He thought Carter would never leave, Carter chatting cheerfully on:

'If you will, Mark, I wish you'd look over some manuscripts for me. I'm in doubt.'

'What, Carter, you don't mean to tell me that you're thinking of letting someone into the closed circle?'

'What are you talking about? We publish at least two new people in every issue.' Mark wished he hadn't started on a subject so passionately discussable.

'I'm very flattered — bring them back tonight'; and he turned to the sheaf of loose papers and began sorting them busily.

'Well, I'm off.' He was gone.

Mark got out of bed and went straight to the telephone book. She would, of course, be under her own name — M-Manning — Elisabeth — George — Hell! The bloody telephone book was never any use when you really wanted something. It was always a number not given, another name. You couldn't even find a laundry when you needed one. It took half an hour to discover that her name was Conti — Manuele Conti. During that time Mark had smoked one cigarette after another. He had called up five different people. He had asked clearly and concisely what he wanted as if it were an important business matter. He had sat on the edge of the bed and decided three times that this was insanity. Far better to go and finish the manuscript, take it to Morton, go to a movie and get Carter to ask some people in after dinner. He thought of the ferret-faced boy, the actor — he would have liked to knock off their heads and watch them bounce down a hill. He hated them all. He hated everybody. He hated that monstrous instrument, the telephone, lying in wait for him. Primrose 4873. PRI——

'Hello? May I speak to Mrs. Conti, please?

'Just a minute. Who is it, please?'

'Mark Taylor — no, not Tyler, Taylor.' She wouldn't remember who he was.

'This is Mrs. Conti.'

'Good morning. This is Mark Taylor.' There was nothing else to say. Apparently there was nothing for her to say either. Eternity stretched from house to house. From city to city. Silence. Emptiness.

'Oh, yes.'

'I wondered if I might come and call before I leave.' 'Before I leave' sounded innocuous enough.

'Well, come to tea this afternoon. That will be very n-nice.'

'About four?'

'About five.'

'Good-bye, then.' She had rung off. This is the way fate is accomplished. It is as simple as that. You pick up a telephone and make an appointment. You are invited to tea. It is done, finished. Mark went to the wall and stood on his head. This was something he had never done in his life before, and he regretted it immediately. The blood rushed to his head. He seemed to have done something to his shoulder. He laughed. God Almighty, it was good to be alive. And now to work.

The mind could only perform its tricks on a tight-rope taut to breaking-point. Everything he had forced himself to write down painfully yesterday, word by word, could be manipulated, tossed lightly here and there, played with, fashioned, because under the fleet-footed mind there now stretched this tautness of emotion. He worked furiously, tearing up pages, rewriting, typing until it was finished, finished and lay there before him in a neat pile. He would mail it to Morton. He would not go through the hell of waiting downstairs, of being ushered in, of facing surprise and the patronizing 'Well done.' At no cost would he jeopardize this fine state of exhilaration, of suspense.

The things one can manage to accomplish in four hours, the hours between one and five that lay between Mark and a street and a house and one person in a room he had never seen — the things one can manage to invent in four hours of complete suspense, are limited. There was lunch to be considered. He sat with one shoe in his hand and considered it not at all. He was extremely hungry, but at this moment as he sat with one shoe in his hand, what he considered, what seized him, was the final shape of his poem. He saw what it would be exactly: whatever had been thrusting itself slowly up out of the dark had chosen this moment to open, and there was nothing to do but accept the fact. Four stanzas stood out complete, as if written on a page in the time it took him to tie his shoe and walk across the room to the desk. (Time telescoped: there is the time of decision, the time of contemplation, the time of creation. They are each different. Sometimes they are all going on at once.) As he wrote, crossing out here and there because sometimes his memory slipped, there was no doubt that more than one stream of time was going on quite distinct one from the other: The things one can manage to accomplish in four hours of complete suspense are unlimited. At the edge of sensation the mind splits up; shot like a rocket, it will explode, and three or four streams of fire burst softly in the dark.

Stars are fixed, their courses unalterable, their burning steadfast. But there are mortal fluids that can leap oceans, erratic human explosions that reach across time — simply from one street in a city to another. Think of London. A warm spring day. There are thousands of women going upstairs now, for it is just after lunch; thousands sighing in the first tiredness of spring; thousands stopping on the second landing a moment to say, 'The hydrangeas in the garden are dying. They should not be in pots any longer'; thousands opening the tall doors of bedrooms, walking across polished floors to the place where the mirror stands (for it is after lunch and they must rearrange their faces, replace the cool mask that the flush of wine has altered). Among the thousands there is also one: Georgia is standing in front of her mirror. She is startled. She is suddenly unaccustomed to the severe outline of her face. It is not often that she observes herself. It is not often that she feels troubled — or perhaps it is simply that there is going to be a thunderstorm. The hand that takes the powder-puff trembles. It is unnatural for that strong painter's hand, used to holding a brush steady in perfect concentration, to tremble at such a light task. It is as if someone were in the room or as if she were expecting someone. The hand that picks up the lipstick and follows the outline of her mouth stops after making the lower lip vermilion — stops as if she were seeing its straight cruel line for the first time, or as if she were aware of someone else's seeing it. But there is no one in the room. The wind blows the curtains out and draws them back again, and Georgia shivers, closing the suddenly vulnerable place with a vermilion outline. There, she is prepared. She is armed. She thinks, it is this warm weather that made me feel a little faint just now. It is the spring. I have been working too hard.

It is afternoon. Still and warm. Warm and still, surprising for April. Mark has been sitting with his head in his hands for almost an hour, and it has not burst, which seems in itself remarkable. It is because he cannot make up his mind to get up and go out, meet people on the street, endure the curious glance of the stranger, and because he is too hungry to think or to be anything but hungry and tired and aching for a meeting that will not take place in time for another two hours. He has suffered the inner explosion, has sent a rocket up, and now is empty like a vessel. He is waiting to be charged. There is the possibility of a drink, a drink which in five minutes can upset the inner mechanism, the delicate balance, and reduce in some curious way the magnetism of the mind. But that escape has served its purpose. It has given him the swan, produced the mirage, and now it is better to have something to eat and go quietly at the appointed time to what waits for him across the city, across the hour.

Suspense is tolerable up to the final moment; then it becomes intolerable. As Mark turned into Clifton Hill Road, as he was faced with the rows of yellow-brick houses one after another with their individual gates, their prim security, it was not possible, he thought, that Georgia Manning lived here. He had got the wrong address. Nobody lived here. It was evident that this was a street where nobody lived, where anybody lived, but not Georgia. Still, here were the numbers, one after another, leading to sixty-three. It was too far, here at one hundred and ninety. No one could endure such a long way. The sun made waves of light in front of his eyes. A rush of embarrassment swept over his face, leaving it hot and red and damp. He could not go in like this. Five minutes to five. It would never do to be late or early. He must arrive at five exactly, the minute upon which his mind had been fixed since ten o'clock this morning, the point on which one end of the tight-rope had been fixed. He stood in the street with his watch in his hand for one minute. Now he would go. He would go, no matter what the time, and if it was three o'clock, never mind.

Sixty-five, a hideous yellow box with turrets — impossible. And then an alley, an arrow pointing down it: sixty-four and sixty-three, studios to the left. A studio to the left presented itself, the Dutch door half-open.

A man in shirtsleeves sat at a round oak table, drawings by Rossetti on the wall. This was a bad dream, a scene in a movie.

'Could you tell me where Georgia Manning's studio is?'

'Her studio is just along there. Her house is just beyond round the corner.' 'Thank you.' He passed a cream-colored door and a dark window at the end of the building, then turned the corner. There it was, in a garden surrounded by grass, a modern house. This was right. He rang the bell. It came over him as the door opened that she might not be alone. If she were not alone he was unprepared. He would have nothing to say. He would have to leave at once.

'Mrs. Conti is in the drawing-room to the left, sir. May I take your hat?'

'Thanks.' From the left there were voices raised a little self-consciously, waiting for whatever should appear following the bell. Hesitating among the others, Georgia's murmured as he came in, 'Yes, it's r-r-rather like a play.'

'Mr. Taylor.' He was standing in the room. There were two others, men, and Georgia, at whom it was impossible to look. There were two other people in the room. Four phrases had been uttered with lightning rapidity by one of the men, and he had not understood one of them. Horror. Until now there had been no element of horror.

'Won't you sit down, Mr. Taylor? H-have some tea? Or sherry?' He found a chair, and now he was in it.

'Yes, please.' Now everything was finished. One could be polite. One could say, 'Two lumps'; one could add, 'No milk, thank you.' The tightrope lay slack on the floor. The mind sat beside it taking off its shoes. He could be easy. He could rest.

'What did I interrupt?' he asked, and was once more attacked by a bubbling sound on his left. In the chair sat a little dark man, leaning forward, bouncing up and down, rushing along like a paper boat on the stream of his own conversation. Suddenly it addressed itself to him. Panic.

'What did you say?'

'I said have you by any chance visited the——' Here he chortled, swallowed, and spluttered for a minute until Mark realized that the end of the sentence had arrived. Georgia was laughing. The other man was laughing. Evidently this was a foreign country. 'Would you mind repeating that in French? I think I could understand it better.' One could choose to be aggressive or one could blush. Mark was so afraid of blushing that he would have rushed at a wild bull at that moment.

'D-don't be embarrassed, Mr. Taylor. Carl is inchomprehensible to most of his friends.'

'He asked if you had ever been to the salt mines. We were talking about Salzburg.' It was the thin, fair boy on the left. It flashed upon Mark that this was no foreign country but simply Oxford. He turned to him gratefully, thinking, Now at last I shall be included.

'No, I never have.'

But at this moment Carl bounced in again, shot off again, spluttering like a firecracker.

'It's most frightfully funny. You get sewn up in a little bag and suspended at a dizzy height on a wire.' He was rocking back and forth, and delivered a speech which was evidently extremely amusing because Georgia, curled up in a corner of the sofa, accompanied it with a steady purr of laughter. But Mark did not understand one word, and began to search for an excuse by which he could leave within the next five minutes. He realized that he was completely unsuited to a social life of any kind. Transparency which he had cultivated so carefully in three months by himself was a liability here. One must perform any feat to avoid reality. Having asked one direct question, the boy in the blue suit had turned away, was leaning forward on his knees, smiling and adding happily to the house of cards.

Mark held his cup on his knee, looking down at it. In a moment he would come to his senses. The unreality of this would vanish. Some tiny maladjustment in the brain would right itself, and he would cease to be a monkey holding frantically to a china cup and become a man in a drawing-room taking part in a conversation.

It was something to be so completely ignored. It happened to him rarely. He could not remember its ever having happened to him to this extent. Often he had wished that he could be present, disembodied on an occasion like this. Here was the opportunity. Here he was in spite of himself merely the observer, the recorder. The fact that on the sofa five feet away was a woman at whose feet he would fall and weep in a simpler world did not alter the case. Mark held his cup on his knee and stirred imaginary tea (for he had long ago drunk it down). The spoon tinkled an accompaniment to what his ear was attending. The tinkling framed the conversation, set it apart on a purely artificial basis. As such, Mark listened to it now as if it were sound without sense.

At Georgia he did not look, he would not yet look. He listened as if to a trio of voices, and observed that it was difficult to distinguish the word or the phrase because it was spoken on an absolutely monotonous level, and divided by shortage of breath rather than by sense. Images came to his mind — the put-put-put of an outboard motor. Georgia's current of laughter was apparently as automatic and continued as Carl's voice. It ran along underneath unpunctuated. Everything apparently was equally amusing in this world. Everything was equally interesting, for they were now talking about French food.

'That absolutely incredible hotel at Macon — you know? On the road to the Riviera, a little dusty town and then this marvelous food — It's so tantalizing, because one is always too tired and too hungry to enjoy it.' Mark was astonished to discover that it was he who had suddenly sprung into the conversation like an automatic doll. He became aware of it only because he was surrounded by silence, and he realized that it was somehow out of key. He had not caught the tune. In the pause he got up and put his cup on the tray. Now he was looking at Georgia's head, and he saw that her hair was faintly red like a Memling madonna and very fine.

Carl bounced up from his cushion and said: 'Georgia, we must be off. We shall miss our train.' Those were not the exact words, but Mark gathered the meaning. With short abrupt movements Carl reached the door. Mark thought, he is a Jew. He is nice. He felt lonely at the sudden perception of this man at whom he had been laughing a moment before. We are different. We shall never find any place to meet in this world. I shall remember him as an outboard motor driving me mad. He will not remember me. The fair boy was shaking his hand.

'Good-bye.'

'Good-bye.'

'S-s-s-sit down. You're not going yet.' She stayed in exactly the same position curled up on the sofa. She lit a cigarette, looking at her hands as she did so. From here you went on, on the same path. There was no other. Sentences rushed through his head, each more banal than the last: 'It's nice of you to ask me to tea' — 'May I have some more tea?' — 'It looks like rain.' These sentences rushed through his mind, but they were unutterable. Let her choose the path. He would follow.

Georgia held an unlit cigarette in her hands. She felt that something was missing. Something had altered with the going out of Carl and David. Now she was here alone with someone she hardly knew. And the air was oppressive. It was going to rain. In a moment he would get up to light her cigarette. In a moment with a gesture she could bridge the pause which was becoming just a little too long. She guessed that he had been uncomfortable for the last half hour. Now she was uncomfortable. She did not know why.

Mark got up and fumbled for the matches in his pocket; found his hand was shaking so that he dropped them on the floor. The blush he had been warding off until now rose like a flood from his heart up through his neck to his eyes. But the matches were there to be picked up.

'Sorry.' She cupped her hands for the light, a curious

gesture, not like a woman's. Glancing at his bent head, she saw that he was scarlet. She was startled to see that he was nervous.

'It's a heavy sort of day, isn't it? Thanks. I f-feel as if something t-t-terrible were hanging over me. But when one feels like that it's always the weather, isn't it? It's never the terrible thing one expects.'

'Oh, one has done rash things because it was a blue day. Only I always foster the illusion that the weather is complementing me, not I the weather. This has been a strange day,' he added, looking at her, but she was not looking at him. She was looking down and smiling.

'Yes, it has. I did nothing at all except order the h-hydrangeas taken out of their pots.'

'I did a terrific amount. I think I must have brought on this thunderstorm. I've been simply blazing away all day.' Now there came an ease between them; because he had spoken for the first time without thinking as one person to another, or because she had looked at him once straight in the eye, a meeting was achieved. A wall slid away. At last he was sitting in a room talking to someone. For three months nothing had been said. Now it was all said. Now he could listen. Now he could talk. What they said, which had been unimportant while the tension existed between them, became important now. Out of talking of what she was doing he could finally ask:

'Why do you have those awful people around? How do you endure them?'

'I'm fond of Carl. I know what you mean, but you see I *can* understand what he says.' (It was not unkind. She smiled.) 'He's brilliant. He's amusing. I should live too much in a feminine world if it were not for f-friends like that.'

'I should go mad. I was on the point of leaving if I had known how to get out, if I had not hoped they would go out first.'

She glanced across at him, wondering what was happening in this room, what was lying so fierily between her and this young man. The thunder in the distance. It sets one on edge. It makes unintended things take on importance.

'You expect such a lot, Mark. May I call you Mark?' So one might ask after a night of love, 'What is your name?' he thought.

'Yes, I expect too much. I have lived too much alone,' he said as she pressed her cigarette into the ash tray. In the pause when anything might have happened, when he might have taken her hand, it was the rain which fell between them, which came between them and made Georgia shiver, made her want to escape the weight of his eyes, the consciousness of his presence. (For why should I be conscious of this young man who is going away?)

'Come and see your landscape before you go.' (Before I go. Before I leave you.) The rain was almost silent, hardly making a sound as it touched the leaves. He followed her out.

'My studio is just round the corner there. We won't get too wet. It is hardly raining at all. See, it is just there.' Her voice hurried along ahead of him. She was walking fast. It was curious that she who had first appeared to him hesitating in a door and moving slowly like a swan through a room full of mirrors, should now be walking fast with her hair coming undone. At the door she turned to wait for him. He was holding out his hands to feel the rain.

'It's nice, isn't it? One feels one has been waiting for this a long t-t-time.' She opened the door.

'I shan't say anything. I never can,' he said quickly.

'You don't need to say anything. There it is.' She pointed to a landscape at the far end of the room. 'I must open the windows, it's so stuffy. I haven't been working today.'

If one can paint the landscape of a mind, this is Georgia's mind, he thought. This is the portrait of a mind — He went over to where it could be seen — Or at least it is the habitat of her mind. It was brown shapes of houses, cool and distinct on either side of a stream. It suggested the South, Italy. In the distance, pale sky, firm brown hills, three thin trees with no leaves on them. These were the elements, but detached they had no more to do with the whole than single notes in a piece of music. The whole was darkness, purity, melancholy. The whole was no real town. The whole was an atmosphere and not a place. He stood looking at it and said:

'It is not an innocent landscape.'

Georgia opened the windows. The heat was stifling, she thought. She looked out. The rain was curiously noiseless. It enclosed the studio and seemed to cut it off. She turned. Mark stood with his back to her. For an instant she thought she must be dreaming: everything looked detached and floating before her eyes. As he turned to speak she was beside him. As he spoke, the words marked themselves like a knife in wax: 'It is not an innocent landscape.'

'I p-p-painted it a long time ago,' she said almost inaudibly. She was thinking, it has been a strange day altogether. It is too hot. The rain is too silent. There is something terrifying.

Mark thought, it is impossible to stay here another minute. Something closes down on us. We are caught. 'May I go on looking?' There were five portraits to be glanced at at decent length. (The afternoon is a slow poison.)

'Do.' (But he is standing too still. He is not really looking. He is not really seeing.) 'Almost everything I have is away — exhibitions and things.'

'I like that,' he said, looking at the portrait of a woman, brilliant and cruel. 'But people must be frightened of you.' Between them lay a desert, a waste of sand. His fingers were of lead, his legs of stone.

It is time this young man with the strained face went, she thought. I am tired. I want to be alone. I want to have time to dress quietly for dinner. It is the silence that is oppressive, the rain making no sound outside, we here, two people who don't know each other. We can't afford to be silent yet. 'Yet' — what are you thinking of? He's going away. He's never coming back.

It thundered, a low, continued roar, and then like the fall of a curtain the big rain came down. Mark had reached the third of the portraits and Georgia spoke quickly, saying one thing after another.

'Listen to the r-r-r-rain.' Now that one had started speaking it was easy to go on. 'Yes, I suppose I do frighten people sometimes. It's so curious; it's not I that's painting really. It's some perception of the eye. I'm surprised at what my own eye sees.'

(If the silence had held for another minute I should have held her in my arms. Now there is no hope. I must go.) Georgia watched him turn toward her, and she felt nervous, though there was no reason to be nervous, she thought. She went on quickly:

'Do you find that with writing — you say things you did not know that you meant until they are said?'

'Yes — often.' They were rising up now as if through water to the air. They were safe. Now he would go to her and say: 'I love you. This has happened to me at last. You will not be able to do anything about it.'

(He is staring at me. He is coming towards me now, and something is going to happen.)

Mark held out his hand. 'I must go now. Thank you so much for letting me come, for letting me see the landscape.' It would be easy to get out now before tears rushed to his eyes.

'It's raining. Will you be all right?'

'Yes, thanks. I'll run for the bus.' What they said was said quickly for fear of something else. At the door he didn't turn.

Georgia stood for a moment at the open door. The rain fell evenly now, making a cool sound on the leaves. She must get dressed for dinner. Nothing had happened. Nothing was wrong that she should want to fall on the ground and weep. I am thirty-five. The landscape is hardly innocent. But is that a reason for wanting to rush out into the rain and fall on my face? Tears have no place here.

As she went out and walked quickly up the path to

the house she denied herself the luxury of tears. She would not cry for no reason. For a boy. For a strange summer day. She would not cry. It was just the rain on her cheek.

Chapter Six

SUSPENSE ends somewhere. Mark's suspense ended once he knew he was out of sight. Then he walked slowly down the street, stopping to ask someone where the bus passed. It was rather pleasant to be getting wet and not to mind, or worry that his only decent suit was getting wet. He sat in the bus pleasantly aware of all that was going on around him. He got off at the proper place and walked to Carter's flat. He walked in and said: 'I'm tired, Carter. I'm going to sleep. Go ahead with whatever you were going to do without me.' He shut the door to his room. Here at last was privacy. He was alone. He lay on his stomach with his face in the pillow. Eventually something would crack inside and he would be all right. Then he could sleep.

Georgia came downstairs in a new dress, for she was persuading herself that whatever had happened or not happened just now in the studio was simply brought about by the heat and had no meaning. So she had put on a new dress that was blue, and as she came down the stairs she called to Manuele:

'Darling, come and look! I have on my new dress.' Her voice changed key — 'Oh!'

'What is it?' Manuele came in and stood at the door.

'That boy. He forgot his hat. What shall we do?' (Stupid of him to leave his hat just there, just now.)

'Well, we'll return it in the morning. It isn't a calamity, after all.'

'No, it isn't a calamity.' (He will have to come back. He will have to come back.)

It was clear. It was simple. He would have to come back. In plays people are always coming downstairs in blue evening dresses and finding a hat in the hall. It is the end of the second act. But I am not an actress. This sort of thing has nothing to do with me, she thought as she took the glass from Manuele's hand and said:

'What sort of day have you had?' She looked at him. This is my husband. This is my love. Here is my peace, my safety, the indestructible part of my life.

'Rather beastly. Mostly arguing with the printer about the Virgil illustrations. You wretched woman, why did you have to do them in color?'

'Mouse, you are being disagreeable. I shall burst into tears.'

'Don't do that. We must go in five minutes. It would never do.'

'You haven't even noticed my dress.'

'I've noticed you. You're looking very beautiful.'

'Mouse,' she said, leaning her head against his shoulder, 'it's been an awful day. I haven't done any work. Only the hydrangeas ——'

'Silly woman, silly woman!' he said, stroking her head with his nervous light fingers. He said 'silly woman' and she did not hear it. She heard: 'You are my wife whom I love, not because you are a painter or because your name is Georgia Manning, but because you are a silly woman, and leave the hydrangeas in their pots much too long.'

'Heavens, Georgia, it's almost half-past eight! We shall be late. Come along, come along, we shall be late.' As they passed through the hall the hat lay on the chair and Georgia's cloak knocked it off. The door slammed shut.

Mark turned over and looked at his watch. Half-past eight. In a moment he would remember something. It had stopped raining. Rain. Oh, yes. Memory comes back like a leak in the lung, like a sharp pain in the chest. Yes, he must go back to the place before he met Georgia and replan, reinvent his life from there. There was a light under the door.

'Carter!'

'Oh, are you awake?' He could have blessed Carter for being there, reason for being there beside these obscure savage emotions. Carter came in. He looked black and solid, outlined against the light.

'Hello, did you have a good sleep? You did look a bit fagged when you came in. Pull yourself together and we'll have a drink,' the voice went on like a pleasant victrola record. 'I have good news for you. Morton telephoned. He's pleased about your article, says it's good and will kick up a hell of a row.'

Mark sat up. Sitting up, he was relieved to find himself back in a life of normal proportions. It is impossible to sustain oneself on a tightrope. He felt hugely relieved, as if he had accomplished a difficult feat and found himself almost miraculously safe upon the ground. Not to have to think about Georgia, to return to a place where one could enjoy one's food, sleep, write articles, put money in one's pocket and hear it jingling pleasantly, reserve a ticket for Belgium.

'It's decent of you to have waited for me, Carter.'

'My motives were interested. You have got to go over these new people with me.'

'O.K., only let's eat.'

'Get your hat.' Hat. Where was it?

'Blast!'

'What's wrong?'

'I left my hat somewhere this afternoon.'

'Well, you can get it tomorrow. It isn't a calamity, after all.'

'No, it isn't a calamity.' He would have to go back.

This time he would go protected. He would go cool with one purpose only. Though she looked like a swan, though he would willingly drive his head into the smooth breast, though he would give much to take the clear face in his hands and hold it quietly and stare to his heart's content — he would give much, but he would not give again what he had given yesterday. He would not give 'body and soul' today; the phrase called up an old piece of jazz. He would go coolly, with the mind carefully adding a tawdry piece of music onto any tendency in itself to burst into song — a seductive piece of music, it must be admitted. He would go protected in more than one way. This was the aftermath, a soft gray day. It was not raining. It was doing nothing positive. The streets were damp but not wet; they did not glisten. Moisture hung in the air; it did not fall. He went straight and unconcernedly to Morton and borrowed five pounds on the article. There were no difficulties. He did not feel cheap. He felt lordly.

He walked through the swinging door at Cook's. He stood like everyone else cursing the slowness of the clerk.

'Yes, a one way ticket to Belgium the day after tomorrow.' Not today, not tomorrow. One must have pause. One must not hurry fate even at the coolest moment of the most indefinite day. The day *after* tomorrow.

'The train leaves at five, did you say? From Victoria?'

'Yes, sir.' A person in an alpaca jacket whose business was tickets bowed.

'Thank you.' He took two pounds out of his wallet.

'It would be cheaper round-trip, sir. The seventeen-day round trip if you are coming back.' You are the devil, no doubt. Cook's is clearly a place where the devil might choose to abide in the form of a bald man in an alpaca jacket luring people back, setting a cry of 'Absence, absence,' in the heart.

'How much cheaper?'

'Well, you'd save ten shillings.' A tenth of my capital would be saved by making this concession. Besides, what if Jean Latour is dead? I can't stay in Belgium forever, however pleasantly one may eat there for however little.

'All right. Seventeen days, you said.'

He had kept the idea of going back to Georgia's well buried under the practical things to be accomplished. Now there was no avoiding it. There was no avoiding the rush of terror, the longing to run the whole way that took possession of him now. 'Curse the woman.' Still, the morning was as remote from the evening as fire from ice. One could never fall on one's knees at eleven o'clock in the morning. He leapt onto a bus. He was on his way.

Georgia left instructions with the maid that when Mr. Taylor called she was to say that Mrs. Conti was working and give him his hat. She was to be firm. Then Georgia walked slowly down the path to the studio. Today she would work. Nothing in the world should stop her from working today. She opened the door — stuffy place, better leave it open. She opened the window. She did all this busily and loudly as if she were doing it for someone else's notice or to convince herself that it was being done. Then she went to the cupboard and drew out the portrait she was working on. It was a nuisance that Tony couldn't come today. It was holding her up frightfully. She put it on the easel and swung it around. She sat on her stool and looked at it. But sitting still other things went on in her mind at the same time. (The background is wrong. Something must be done to the color there. It jumps out. How much of yesterday did I dream? Or what that I dreamed last night took place? What has happened? I have never in my life had a clear dream of love. But the fact that I dreamed it is the absolute proof that it will never happen. Things that one dreams never happen. I am ten years older than he, at least. What are you thinking of? It always feels cheap to wake up out of a dream. She could not bear the thought of seeing him again. As if she knew things about him that he did not know himself, as if she had surprised him naked and asleep in the night, or as if he had been drugged and had made love to her without knowing what he was doing. If he should walk in now it would be as a man who has made love to me without knowing it. It would be unendurable — but the background, the background is wrong. The whole thing is rotten. I am falling off. I shall never be able to work today.) She took it off the easel and put it with its face to the wall. But this was worse. Now the room was empty. Now at any minute he might go past the door. She climbed onto the stool and sat looking at the long cross-bars of the easel. Would he go by twice, once on his way to the house and once on his way back, and not come in? (Stop thinking, you fool. The leaves themselves seem to be waiting. They lie one on top of the other like painted leaves. The rain does not fall. The elements conspire against me now.)

Mark stood in the door. She did not have time to look away, and he was caught, just as she was, in the moment so long expected, caught unaware and startled out of any semblance.

'You have come back for your h-h-hat.' (Now the unreal becomes real. This is the dream. He is standing in the door. He is here.)

'Yes, you're working. I won't stay.' (She is blushing. The real becomes unreal. The careful preparation crumbles. She is blushing. I am dreaming now.)

He was standing beside her. There was nothing to do except to stand and look down at the hand on her lap, stand and let the dream take possession slowly of his body, atom by atom. Quietly and certainly, without hesitation, almost without desire as a magnet draws up the needle of a compass, his hand closed on hers. It was done: the infinite confined now within ten fingers. Love has set its absolute limit on them. They are bound.

'How long it has seemed.' (I have spoken. I have said something. Perhaps too soon. There is no way of knowing where we are now, what she is thinking.) She is not thinking. She is waiting. They are both waiting. So a man climbing the icy slope of a mountain waits a second with his foot on a tiny ledge, waits intent for the next step, for the next place where he can set his hand, his foot, and not fall. But there is only one way on from here.

Superb the unfaltering instinct, the command of the senses that turns his head down to her throat, his mouth swift and certain to her throat. There, it is accomplished. It is enough. The hands fall. They stand apart.

'You are a stormy petrel.' The cool, ironic voice closes the open space.

'Am I?' The words have no meaning. They are a ritual to be accomplished, the means of bridging a space. 'There is nowhere to go from here.' (Nowhere because the day after tomorrow I shall be gone. Because you are married. Because there is no place on earth where I can take you peacefully in my arms. Because this is the beginning of a nightmare.)

'No.' She sat on the stool looking down at the hands in her lap, looking down at the hands lying helplessly in her lap as if they were not hers. (Nothing to do now but wait, wait for what will make the leaves stir, the rain fall. I have no part in this. It will happen as it must.)

'You must get off that stool. You are too far away.' She will get off. She will obey for this is the dream. She will follow. Now they are standing face to face. They are on top of the mountain.

'My peace, my peace.' (This is real. This is the end of dreaming.)

'I'm afraid I shall disappoint you.'

'How? Why? You can't disappoint me. You can't alter this.' Is she thinking of him or of Manuele? Is she thinking of beds in hotel rooms? But she can add or take away one thing only. She can let the tree flower or lop off the leaves and branches: the root is there.

'No, it's not that. I'm simple, you'll find.' (That is not it. I am not simple. But in this I am simple and in this he is complicated. I am settled. I am not to be torn apart. I can take what is offered. I can be happy.)

'I am complicated.' (But it is not true. I am simple. I am simply a fountain springing suddenly out of the rock. I do not ask anything but to be as I am. I shall not be happy. It is a reality and not a dream. It is not something I must make. It is something that will make me.)

He was not aware of the silence or that his head had been hard against her for a long time until she stumbled. Now they were woken up out of the trance. It was time to begin remembering. The past was already growing behind them, unexplored.

'Come and sit down. Let's talk. Do you remember?' They were sitting on the little green sofa in the corner. 'Do you remember the Café Royale?' She nodded, looking down, the curious sidelong glance.

'I thought you looked like a swan.'

'Did you?' She is looking down.

'You must look at me, Georgia. You must let me look at you.' (For I don't know her. I hardly know her.)

(I don't want to look at him. This is happening too quickly. I want to hide a little longer. I do not want to be exposed. I do not want to be found out. I do not want to give myself away to this young man whom I don't know, whom perhaps I don't want to know.)

(This face I hold in my hands is a mask. The clear gravity of the eyelids, the heavy stillness of it, for it is not a light face with the nerves apparent in its outline. It is a carved face.) He looked down at the mouth, dropping his hands he looked down at the mouth. 'You have a cruel mouth — cruel, cruel,' he said, kissing her for the first time.

Now it is here. At last the door is unlocked. I am not afraid, she thought, opening her eyes and meeting his, first one and then the other.

They must look a long time: years would not be enough. (Here she is, then. Here is the woman behind this created face. The small glancing eyes, the shutter of the eyelid half closed — all this, open now, as clear as ice, the bottomless pupil opening and opening. This is a secret. She has a secret face and this is its secret. This strange purity.)

(He is young. It is not I he is seeing but himself. He is pleading with himself, not with me. He is my child. He is my cherished one, not to be hurt.)

So grave, she looked as one might look faced with death. The long, clear glance, the absolute of it could not be endured. His eyes dropped. His head turned to her shoulder.

'My child, my child.' As she spoke her hand stroked his hair. 'Your hair is black,' she said, lifting herself from the waist so that she became in an instant very tall. It was an instinctive, a personal gesture, but it had the terrible grace of a moment in a Greek play. It had the suspense before fate in it. It contained no pity.

'My child, my child.' (Yes, I am your child.) As she said it, as the fingers stroked his hair softly and impersonally, for the first time in years he thought of his mother simply, his mother whom he would not allow himself to remember, now she was here. With his eyes shut he was leaning against her breast. He would look up to find her red hair, her white white skin that was so soft. How jealous he had been of her! He remembered lying in bed waiting for her to come home from a party. He remembered thinking he would punish her and pretend to be dead when she came in. And he had lain painfully holding his breath. She came in with his father and said, 'Look, he's asleep,' and there at the foot of his bed there had been a long silence and his mother had made a little moaning sound and said in a strange husky voice he had never heard, 'Come along.' When the door shut he had sobbed and beaten his fists on the pillow. He had sobbed loudly, but nobody came. She did not hear. She had forgotten him. And out of the hatred and anger he had felt twenty years ago and the loneliness he said savagely:

'I'm not your child.' He got up and walked away to the window. 'Why do you call me your child?'

'I meant that you were sweet and ch-cherished, darling.' (That he cannot understand. He does not know what it is, the sharp pain in the chest; this is a woman's tenderness. He cannot understand it. He is furious at being made a child of. He does not see that I am carrying him now in the most secret part of myself, and that he is being born in the womb.)

'Georgia, Georgia, you will be honest with me. Whatever happens. You will tell me the truth.'

'Yes, I will.'

'We hardly know each other. It's so strange.'

'I know.'

'I have so little to offer you. I'm afraid. I'm afraid of not being able to go on.'

'You're beautiful. You will go on being that.' (Beauty, hideous word. It's not I that you love, then. It's something else. I have nothing to do with it, the small tense hands, the black hair — these are not I. Love me for some hideous quality, for some vice, for some secret despair that we share, but not for that.)

'What a thing to say to a man — it's unforgivable.'

'You are a funny creature — you are sweet.'

'It's raining again. It always rains when we meet.'

'It has rained the twice we have met, if that proves anything.'

'Georgia, Georgia, who are you?' But this she will not answer. This must be turned aside or asked in another way. It cannot be discovered in a caress. This is a question one does not answer, for it is unanswerable. Carefully and precisely and hardly thinking what she was doing, she took his fingers one by one and pressed them.

'Come tomorrow. Come to see me before I go at my friend's flat.'

'Yes, I'll do that. That is possible.' (We will not think beyond tomorrow yet. We will not go beyond this moment.)

'You have nice hands, Mark.' It is time to go. It is time he went. Love like this is a liqueur; one can have too much of it. She thought of her house, of the flowers to be arranged, of the work to be done, of the people coming to tea, of Manuele. The vacuum in which they had been held exploded and they were back in the world, each in his separate world.

'My darling, you must go now.' (She is already asking me to go. This is the beginning of the nightmare, that I must never stay, that from now on each time we must reascend the mountain, and when we have reached the peak there is nowhere to turn but down.)

'All right. All right.' He got up so that he could bend down and hold her well in his arms. (For this moment you are mine.)

'Go, go.' (I do not want any more to be quite swept out into these foreign places. I want to be here where I am, at home. I do not want to be seized and shaken. There are things to be done.)

'I'm going. I'm going.'

How does one go? Who suddenly takes command and says to the unwilling hand 'Drop,' to the bending torso 'Lift,' to the heavy head 'Wake'? Panic took him. (I shall not be able to leave. I shall cry out. I shall be turned to salt.) But already the violence of parting was accomplished. In the secret cry of despair it was already accepted.

'There, I have gone.' He stood in the door. 'You don't know the address. It is Taviton Street 44. His name is Carter. You won't forget.'

'When?'

'Three o'clock.' (Don't go. But it is I who said 'Go,' who have made him go.) 'Be happy, darling.' She came to the door. (Happiness. Happiness has nothing to with this. Happiness is something else.) He was gone.

He walked quickly down the street. (Happiness is her word, not mine. Happiness is hers. I don't want it. Or at least my happiness is not this. It is lying on my stomach in the grass on a hot day. It is not this flood in the heart.)

She stood in the door resting against the wood frame, resting heavily against it. (It is raining.)

In this way, and articulating in her mind only words like this, would she admit the secret: 'It is raining.' That is as far as she would allow herself to say 'I am in love.' She would go no further. She would quickly take refuge in the chairs and tables, in the flowers to be arranged. She would not try to discover the reason of why she had done no work; or it was because Tony hadn't come. She must ask Catherine to telephone and find out when he could make up for this lost morning. She shut the door of the studio and did not look back. There before her stood her house. Quickly and firmly she walked toward it, opened the door, and walked into the cool, green hall. It was only when she saw the hat on the chair that she thought with panic, 'I have promised to go and see him tomorrow.'

Chapter Seven

MARK turned over on his back and opened his eyes. It was light already, morning already. He felt as if he had spent the night on a tiresome train journey, stopping and changing every half hour, he had so many small fruitless dreams. He had not dreamed of Georgia, he had dreamed of his hat floating down a river. He had dreamed an exact dream of buying a ticket for a place the man had never heard of and shouting 'Latour! Latour!' at him to no purpose. It was a relief to see the light. He looked at his watch. Four o'clock. He got up and went to the window. The street lamp outside looked like a red sun rising out of water. (They should turn them off when it is so light.) In a tree in the street the wood pigeons cooed insistently, persistently, in an unchanging soft monotone. (They are trying to make a different sound but can't. Their voices always go back to the same 'rou-cou' even though they are trying to say something quite different.) He was wide awake. As he stood at the window looking out in the cold clear light it was more resting than that troubled sleep had been. At this hour the blood is turned to water; the mind floats easily upon it. He stood at the window and looked at the unchanging light and was glad to be awake.

He surveyed the last two days and the immediate future. It lay there like a map before him, the limits fairly drawn, the cities and villages there to be observed. It astonished him that he rebelled so little at the facts. Here is a country where I can go, the small mountainous country where Georgia and I will meet at long intervals and stand for a moment on the peaks looking down. Here are the great peaceful plains where I am not allowed: the rhythm of days and nights following each other, the falling asleep listening to the rain, the waking up to say, 'Have you had a good night?' We shall never have time to be simple and easy with each other.

But, he thought, looking at the solitary workman bicycling across the city with his bag, in another way I have come home. I am accepted. I am known and accepted. The years before this event seem interminable looking back now.

He thought of his childhood, the tiny blue room in the house in Paris where he had lain pretending to be dead. The strange sinister atmosphere, tropic, as if there were always a storm on its way, his beautiful passionate mother, his father whom he had hated, of whom he had been so jealous. His childhood had been a childhood in a foreign country. It had never been home. It had been a place of devastating lonely emotions ending — only in this unnatural morning light would he allow himself to remember it — ending with the day when he had seen his father strike his mother with his fist. Then he had been taken away. He had been given away. He had been released mercifully from learning anything more.

He thought of Nice — the great impersonal house where he only felt comfortable in the kitchen playing hearts with Marie. Bundy, whom he mistrusted because she lied about his mother and told him she was dead when he knew she wasn't, piecing together the torn envelopes in the waste-basket. Bundy showed him off to her friends and made him wear starched white sailor suits. During all this time, from when he was seven to when he was nineteen and ran away, certain phrases recurred nightmarishly. 'Mark, go and wash your hands. The Comte de Ségur is coming to lunch. Be sure to address him properly.' — 'Mark, go upstairs and get a handkerchief for me like a good boy.' And then, as he grew older, 'Mark, where *have* you been?'

He thought of Jeannette, whom he had had a brief affair with the summer he ran away. It was she who lent him the money. And then Paris, a dream in bright garish colors, his queer unsatisfactory relationship with Al and the break at the end. There was his life with one single thread of the same color running through it, his being sure he could write.

Now at last he had come home. Now he had found someone with whom he could lie and find a temporary peace at last. The whole freight of the miracle swept over him in the early light. Something is solved now: I am alive.

The street lamps suddenly went out, making the world gray and cold. But it did not matter. Mark went back to his bed and turned over to shut out the light. For the first time in years he repeated the Lord's Prayer. Then he fell asleep, deep asleep, without moving, as if he had been blessed.

When he woke up it was ten o'clock. Carter had gone, leaving a note to say that coffee was on the stove. He went to the window to look out at the street and the lamp. But now the sun divided it into light and shadow. People hurried along it; taxis bustled noisily up and down. The trees looked dusty and bright. Only the wood pigeons were cooing still without impatience, softly and persistently — 'for love is stronger than death,' he laughed, and went into the kitchen to get some breakfast.

Across the city Georgia was sitting in the warm studio squeezing gobs of magenta and orange paint onto the palette on her arm. In a moment Tony would be there. This, she felt in her bones, would be a good day. Looking at the portrait on the easel she knew exactly what she would do with it. Looking at it she thought: 'I shall heighten it all instead of subduing it. I was mad to think it needed sobering.' Thinking this in the brilliant morning light, she was also penetrated with sweetness. She was not thinking it, but she knew. It did not need to be phrased. It was there like a warm flood inside her, flowing regularly from one central point through her arms and down to the powerful hands, powerful this morning. One can live for a long time in the dark, and then suddenly there is a lamp lighted. The eye sees. The mind burns. The vision is apparent.

'I'm sorry I'm late.' In came Tony in his yellow shirt, with his woolly red hair standing up. 'Have you decided what you are going to do? Is this all right?' he said, climbing up onto the dais and the chair and arranging his hand along it.

'Don't bother about your hand, Tony. I shan't be working on it today.' Already she was looking at him abstractly and impersonally.

'You *are* looking severe this morning.'

'Am I? Tony, my dear, I can't talk this morning. I really must get this finished.'

'All right. I'll be as silent as the grave.' (Nice boy. There! That's much better already.) She half shut her eyes. One point of color, of impossible brilliant color after another, and then suddenly it was light, atmosphere, and not points of color any more. (There, there, there! It's living. It's coming alive.)

Mark sat at the desk looking at the ugly brown wall with the inkstand on it. Already he had torn up three drafts of a letter to Jean Latour. The image of an old minister of agriculture kept coming between him and what he wanted to say, and then the tenses kept getting mixed up. Damn the imperfect subjunctive! He began again:

'Cher Monsieur: Some two months ago I discovered a volume of your poems at the house of a friend. I am myself a poet, and happened to be living there alone at work on a long poem. It has meant so much to me that I wondered if I might make so bold as to call on you. I shall be in Ghent on Friday for some time and can be reached poste restante. Acceptez mon hommage, cher Monsieur, et croyez à mes sentiments les plus distingués.' — Signed, Mark Taylor.

There! That would have to do. He opened the fly leaf of the book and addressed it to the printer in Ghent: 'Please forward.' (Of course there is not the slightest reason to think he is living in Ghent after all.) He took out a sheet of paper and wrote also to the printer, asking him to forward him Jean Latour's address if he were still living. He licked the envelope and stamped it down with his hand. Then he turned in his chair.

Georgia is coming here! In spite of his early morning conviction that everything was good and all right, still nothing could be good enough or certain enough to be armed against atmosphere. How many things that might have happened have not happened because a darkening in the sky has seemed too ominous; how many bitter quarrels have taken place in hotel rooms because of a mouldy smell and the grime on the edge of the curtains. This room was worse because it was not impersonal. It was Carter's room.

He examined it: the dingy wall that had been beige but needed repainting, the amateur oil portrait of Carter unframed over the mantel, the gas stove, the shelves of books piled on top of each other, the sad-looking armchairs he must have bought second hand, the studio couch with the pillows arranged over a torn place. The sun pouring in makes it worse, he thought. I shall have to clean this place. The idea of cleaning it came as an inspiration. It would keep him from thinking. It was an action definitely related to the afternoon. 'Where in hell does Carter keep his brooms and things?' He finally dragged out an old broom and a piece of torn shirt and raised a dust-storm on the carpet. He nearly choked until he thought of opening the window. But it was fun. It was better than sitting with his hands as cold as ice imagining things. When he had swept, he sat down on the floor and began arranging the books — there was lots of poetry. He sat, reading here and there, as he stacked them up in rows. Opening a dusty red-covered Matthew Arnold he was startled to read:

> Children dear, was it yesterday?

Sitting on the floor with the book on his knee he came across that line, the poem which as a child he had kept as a secret, a secret woe to be recited over and over like an incantation. Now it was here, making the moment and the day intolerable with its ache:

> Call her once before you go —
> Call once yet!
> In a voice that she will know:
> 'Margaret! Margaret!'
> Children's voices should be dear
> (Call once more) to a mother's ear;
> Children's voices, wild with pain —
> Surely she will come again!
> Call her once and come away;
> This way, this way!
> 'Mother dear, we cannot stay!
> The wild white horses foam and fret!'
> Margaret! Margaret!

This he had said over and over lying in the grass on his stomach, lying far up on the warm stones looking down over the sea. Now here it was, remembrance sharp as a whip, leaving a scarlet thread where it stung. Georgia — Georgia, the temporary sweetness, the illusion of permanence and peace. He might pretend, but it would always be a matter like this of rooms not their own, of strange places, of scenes to be played. It would always be a pathetic imitation. She would always get up and go. She would think, 'I must go home.' (You damn fool, to think for a moment that you could make roots here, that you could ever be anything, hold anything true here. Take it for what it is, the resolving chord of a little tune you heard in the Café Royale, but get out while you can, before what's left of your immortal soul dissipates itself in a day dream.) 'You damn fool' was audible. It pulled him up on his feet and set the red book back on its shelf. It destroyed the peace of the early morning completely. It is possible, he thought as he looked absent-mindedly for his hat, to be as lonely as one has ever been in five minutes in a strange room.

But his hat, his hat was not to be found. He had left it at Georgia's. One goes back to get one's hat and leaves instead what little wit one had, the head on one's shoulders.

He looked at the dingy room. The sun was behind a cloud. It was the place chosen for a meeting. It looked gray and nondescript, nothing worse. Here in an hour or so his hat would be returned to him and he would take his leave for another country. Meanwhile he would go out and get some lunch and maybe some flowers. And he would stamp the letter to Jean Latour and mail it.

Georgia put down her palette and pressed the palms of her hands into her eyes to cool them.

'There, Tony, it's finished — and I'm finished,' she said, jumping off the stool. 'You have been angelic. Come and have a sherry. Come and talk to me.' She would not look at the portrait again until after lunch.

It whirled in front of her eyes. But Tony was standing in front of it scratching his head.

'It's violent, all right. But I think I like it.'

'I don't know. I can't see it yet. Come along. Let's get out of this smell of paint. How hot it is! Come along, Tony,' she said, pulling his arm, pulling him away. She would carefully not think any further than the next two hours. When she was a child she had played a game of never walking on the cracks in the pavement outside their house. If one walked on a line something terrible would happen. Now this was a game. If she thought at all about the afternoon, about Mark, it would be like dreaming. It would spoil something.

Three o'clock in the afternoon, the lowest ebb in the tide of the day. The dazzle on the pavement was frightful. Georgia did not know where to look. She felt that this was an interminable journey. She wished she had never come. She wished she were anywhere but walking along a street in the middle of the afternoon. She wished she were sitting in the dank dark parlor of any one of the small hotels reading *Punch.* She did not consider where she was going; she thought only of arriving somewhere and sitting down in the dark.

A second, five minutes, an hour: these are measures. They do not measure the time it takes to go from one house to another. They do not measure the time it takes for the spirit to slip down to zero like mercury, for a man to sit with his head in his hands wishing he were anywhere but in a brown room waiting for another man's wife. Luckily it is time and not eternity. Time is elastic, but it has a beginning and an end. Someone knocked at the door.

'It's you! How did you find your way up?'

'By intuition — and because Carter's name is on the door.' She took off her hat. 'I'm here. I thought I should never get here.' She was blinking with the sudden change of light, an impression of dinginess, a smell of roses and tobacco. 'There are r-r-r-roses somewhere.'

'Yes, over there. They're almost falling.'

'It's like summer.' She took out her compact. 'My dear, I'm so *hot*,' she murmured.

'I'll get you a glass of water.' Anything to get away for a moment and try to break the ring of silence, the numbed feeling that got him when she walked in and he could only think: This is unsuitable. It's too light. There is nothing to say. There is nothing to do. When he came back she had lit a cigarette.

'Thanks. I'm beginning to see again. What have you been doing all m-m-morning?'

'Oh, pottering about. I wrote some letters. And you?' He was sitting on the arm of the chair opposite her.

'I finished a portrait.' Why had she come? Why were they sitting here talking to each other across an abyss?

'Good?'

'I haven't dared look at it yet.' She had been working away all morning, he thought angrily. (I have nothing to say. There is going to be a silence, an unbearable silence.) She was looking down, looking down at her hand as if it belonged to somebody else.

'I love you. I love you,' he said loudly into the emptiness. They were the only words that came into his head. They resounded in the room with finality. They fell on the floor and lay there. He regretted them, but could not call them back now.

(He shouldn't have said that just then. There is something wrong about this room, about this afternoon.)

(It would be so easy to go over and take her hand now. Once that is done the silences will have no importance. They will be part of the words — they will be the words. If she were someone else — but it is not this that I want. It is knowledge, he thought, clenching his fist on his knee. I do not want to make love to her. I want her to open a door in her breast and let me see her heart like a Dali painting.)

'Why are you smiling?'

'I was thinking if you were someone else this would be easy, this hellish afternoon,' he said, going up to the curtains and pulling them closed with a rasping sound 'That's better.'

'You are a strange boy.'

'Am I so strange?' he said, leaping now into the situation plain before him. (There is no other way You are caught. You are a man. She is a woman.) He would have to take the easy substitute. He would never know her better than in the moment of going over and taking her two hands. There were the clear eyes, open, unwavering.

'How impersonal eyes are!' he said bitterly, blotting them out, shutting out the painful thinking, the frozen, aware, seeking mind, letting his senses take possession of him, letting the slow kiss open a different door — not the heart, not the heart.

'Yes, I know, you have to go now. For the last half hour I have been waiting for you to say that.' (But nothing has happened. We are the same two people who sat here before. We have been on a journey and come back.)

'You are a black cat,' she said pulling his ears.

'Don't pull my ears, you beast.'

'Nice ears.' (These are the comfortable places where we shall live and know each other from now on. Here is our charming perfect little world where we might be two teddy bears, where we are too sweet for words.) But she was stroking his ears.

'I know. You're going. You're going,' he said, looking down at her, looking down into her eyes. (Is this your secret, that you have none?) Georgia, you'll write? You won't forget me?'

'I'll write.' She would write him letters — another avenue of discovery, another continent of the mind to be explored. He pulled her up with one hand.

'Bless you, bless you.'

'I think I shall paint another landscape.' (He is going to be lonely. Bound to be. He is sweet standing there holding my dress in his hands. I shall miss him.)

'Oh, darling, what are those silly little creatures on your dress?' It was green and white with a pattern all over it.

'Goats,' she said in a curious deep voice, 'goats.' As she said it he thought: This is going to haunt me. It's a word like fate. It had to be spoken here in this beastly room.

'You mustn't forget the roses,' he said aloud. 'They are falling.'

'It has been a warm afternoon.'

'A lovely afternoon.' (But it has not been a tea after all.) 'You will write. You will write.'

'Promise.' He watched her go down the stairs slowly like a swan. (She can't go like this. Nothing is said. I don't know. I don't know her, he thought.) 'I'm coming with you, Georgia — wait!' he shouted.

'Why, darling, you look as white as a sheet. What's the matter?' He held her two arms hard in his hands.

'Don't go,' he begged. 'Don't go and leave me alone here.'

He was as high-strung as a bow, she thought. Poor child. Poor darling. 'There, there! Let go, my sweet.' She took his head in her hands. She kissed his eyes and his mouth. 'I must go. But I'll write. I'll write,' she promised. 'Be happy, my darling.'

'Are *you?* Are *you?*' For he must have some assurance, now she was going away. He must know. Her eyes opened wide and let him look down as far as he could. She nodded.

'That's all right, then.' He leaned his head on her shoulder for a moment as if out of the core of confusion, the departure, the cries and shouts of anguish that were beating around him, he could still hold to that peace.

She said again: 'I must go. I must go.' She felt that it would be indecent to stay another second. Something here was exposed too raw. They would at any moment burst into tears. This piercing sweetness would suddenly become papier-mâché, love a doll in their hands. With instinct rather than thought she left him quickly before there was time for a last word. The door shut behind her.

Mark stood looking through the glass and watched her go. She did not turn. She looked once up at the house and then disappeared into a taxi. Sometimes there is no space for pain. The severed limb maintains the illusion of its own existence. The ache comes later. He ran up the stairs, ran back into the room, and flung himself down on the bed. Not to know. Not to feel. To forget.

Georgia hailed a taxi. Looking up at the house, Mark, she thought, is somewhere inside this strange house.

'Sixty-three Clifton Hill Road.' She took off her hat and leaned her head against the back of the seat, though it wobbled from side to side.

'This is life,' she thought, this wanting to shut one's eyes and let one's head fall where it would; this being relaxed and very tired was love, she supposed. Lurking somewhere in the back of her mind was the inevitable monster, remorse. There is nothing worse in the end for the soul than to have to accept these burdens of love. She thrust the pang away that he would inevitably suffer, suffer more than she. For I am incredibly lucky, she thought, leaning back in the corner looking out. There is Manuele; there is all the pattern of my life; there is my work. I am in no danger, she thought, but he is in danger. He has not learned to accept the pattern of things. He will want to smash it. Suddenly she felt relieved, so relieved that she blushed with the shock, that she would not ever be faced with living with Mark. It was shameful. One should want to live with the people one loved. She thought of the long rhythm of her days and nights with Manuele. She thought of cooking for Mark some day in a cabin in the mountains, of sleeping in the grass with him, but not life with him.

Living was this. It was Manuele. It was Mark. Am I being cynical? Is this cruelty? Is it cruel to be as one is? But he is going away, thank God, he is going away. I shall not have to face the possibility of his suffering. I shall not suffer very much myself. It is there. It has happened and I am so tired, so mortally tired, she thought, trying to get her bag open as she got out of the taxi, and dropping her gloves. Exasperating little men, taxi drivers. They haven't an atom of gallantry in them. As she stooped to pick them up her head whirled. It would be absurd to end the afternoon by sitting down in the street. She was startled and abashed by this weakness. It was a drink she needed. She needed to tell Manuele that she had nearly fainted in the street and wasn't it absurd? She must be getting old.

Chapter Eight

MARK'S packing was simple and efficient. It consisted of Jean Latour's book, his own manuscript, various sizes of pads, three clean shirts, two pairs of pajamas, his gray suit that needed pressing — hat, hat. Well, well, well, there was clearly nothing to do but go and fetch it. Hours before his train left. Clearly he must have a hat to cross the Channel with. Clearly he must be armed with a hat if Jean Latour turned out to be Minister of Agriculture.

For the third time he walked toward the white house in the green square of grass. In this play there are three acts. But it did not occur to him as he walked soundlessly across the grass that the third act might take place in silence. The studio was locked. The front door of the house was open as if someone had just gone out for a minute. Mark rang, and walked into the drawing-room. No one. It looked cool, empty, and clean. The ash trays lay in their places, immaculate. The flowers, larkspur against beech leaves, looked as if they had just been arranged; they stood stiffly at attention. In a bowl on a table wide-open peonies showed their yellow hearts. Into this formal stage Mark walked looking for his hat. It would not be here, but he would wait here, he thought, sitting down, until someone came who could tell him where it was. The thought that Georgia might be somewhere upstairs in a room he had never seen added to his sensation of being wild, a wild creature strayed into a room. He sat on the edge of the sofa starting at the loud scratch of his match on the box. No one, apparently, was going to answer the door. He was not expected; he was actually in the mind of Georgia already gone, already somewhere in the middle of the sea. He was, in fact, not here at all.

Sitting in this particular room following the events of the past week he felt extraordinarily stimulated. It was absolutely still, and as he sat and listened he became quite certain that the house too was empty. He was alone. He was alone and free. Free because he was here in Georgia's house — and alone.

It is always in the end, he thought, to these still moments that one returns: after the journeying, to the small house on the hill; after the tempest, to the calm, the blue oil of the sea. And always, he thought, it is some dream of a quiet country that leads one to these passionate journeys — to be eternally deceived. Because the peace is the antithesis of the journey. It is the coming home, not the departing. It is in remembering a landscape that it takes on peace. But here he was not deceived. Here in this room were all the elements of passion, but arranged for contemplation instead of action. Here was the quiet country that had been so lacking yesterday, had been so lacking in the night when he had been incapable of thought but only pursued by the kaleidoscope of meaningless images that the tired mind threw up like seaweed on the beach.

For Georgia was here far more than she had been in the moment of surrender, in the moment of sitting down in Carter's room and taking off her hat. There was more to be found of her, he guessed, in the arrangement of the chairs, in the landscape on the wall, than a hand under her breast would discover or the more secret organs of the body ever touch. Here in this empty and absolutely silent house lay the knowledge for which he had cried out when he said, 'It is not intimacy but knowledge — *who are you?*' Now he would find her.

He sat quite still and looked and felt out the room. First, its formal quality: everything here spoke of detachment, a room set like a stage for an audience of one person. In that corner of the sofa sits Georgia, he thought, and this is the stage — these huge windows making the trees more important than the chairs, the weather more important than the conversation, the diminishing mirror on the mantel providing escape for the mind, giving the threatening entrance its minimum proportion. The mirror is her mind reducing the vague impression, the involuntary wave of emotion, to a small exact image of a scene. The mirror is the mind of the room. The flowers are its spirit: dark purple and blue larkspur against the unpleasant green-brown shiny copper beech, a deliberate discord, an accepted conflict; the peonies, a calm voluptuousness content in its mystery. Nowhere in this room is there visible Georgia's heart. She is the audience. She does not play here. In the end it is a cold room for that reason. It lacks a secret. One is exposed here to the trained eye, to the curious mind, he thought.

He hesitated to leave a cigarette, a trace of his passing. For I am not really here, I am on my way to Belgium. He got up and threw it out of the window. The front door was still open. He looked quickly and methodically round the hall — yes, there under the chair, curious place to find a hat. In a second he had it in his hand and was gone. I shall never know, he thought, whether I dreamed this or whether it really happened. For now I am on my way to Belgium.

Of Georgia what he knew, what he had found was a landscape seen long ago and the touch, the quality, the shape of an eyelid — nothing more. What he guessed at through sitting ten minutes in her empty house was a need for secrecy, a shutness of personality, a need to keep certain things in herself unexplored, unknown. Was it that that gave her painting an impression of both hiding and revealing something? There, in a point of magenta, in the strange purple of a shadow under the tree might be divined the summer afternoon when she had felt desire at the bottom of her spine like a poison; there in the cool planes of the houses lay a certain negation of her mind, its love of order; there, in the torrent, the fury in her heart which could give the swan lift to her head. She must, sometimes, have drawn back, have wanted to tear up a canvas once it was finished. And this curious tension between the tyranny of the art and her temperament gave excitement and point to everything she did.

All this Mark saw clearly. He was thinking so hard that he performed the actions of departure mechanically, leaving a note for Carter and half a crown for the maid on the bureau. And as he saw all this he saw also that his passionate desire to know her was wrong —

love, an extraneous quality, complete in itself, giving no right to expect anything further nor outside itself. At least in this case. And yet I can't help it, for it is not love I want but knowledge, he thought, snapping the bag shut and lifting it off the bed with an impatient gesture, picking up his hat and leaving, leaving the apartment and London, running down the stairs pursued by his thoughts, which would not allow him to go in peace.

When he was a boy his tutor had picked up a crab on the beach and forced the plates of the belly apart to show him the reproductive organs. Now he remembered it: the shiver of excitement as the penknife cut into the crack and lifted it open as if it were a great weight, that locked door. He had screamed, 'Don't! Don't!' as it was forced open and his tutor laughed. 'It doesn't really hurt him, you know, though he is putting up such a fight.'

So now, sitting finally in a corner of a compartment in the train, he had a sense of criminal flight. That is what I wanted to do to Georgia, he thought. And yet I have committed no crime — looking at the headline 'Farmer confesses to rape of ten-year-old girl.' I have raped no one.

Without preparation, without reason, as one might take a bird in the hand, he had wanted to seize Georgia, possess her completely in one way or another — and every way had failed, the simple way of the hand and mouth, the subtle way of the imagination. I am wrong, he decided, I am in some way wrong in everything I have done except this, except this going to Belgium. Belgium, the thing he still felt certain about, with the certainty of a compass finding its north.

THE SINGLE HOUND

PART III

Chapter One

ONCE on the channel boat, sitting in the bar with a glass of beer, looking through the open door at the hazy, shiny, still sea, Mark felt the tension of the last weeks fall slack. The effect of a body of water is as strong as a temporary loss of memory: when one reaches land on the other side some physical virtue has gone out of the past. One is merely remembering something that has happened. It is not any longer the peculiar personal ache in the limbs. He was already existing in the immediacy of the journey, listening to the three middle-aged Englishwomen doing their accounts beside him and wondering how much to tip the porter — amused at the inability of the French to dress 'pour le sport,' as exemplified by a woman in a large floppy hat and a checked brown and white coat which flapped in the wind, absorbing her whole attention. When Mark had finished his beer he went down into the men's smoking-room and slept.

He woke up startled to find that the brown shore with its line of hideous hotels lay in sight. Now he was within ten minutes of that country whose name he had said over and over like a charm in so many situations. 'I am going to Belgium,' he had said to Carter's friends, as if that might explain why he could never write a play about Matteotti, why he would never go to see the ferret-faced boy in his nice flat. 'Tomorrow I shall be gone,' he had said to Georgia, meaning you need not be afraid, meaning let us take this moment while it is here. In imagination it had been so many things; now he was within a hundred miles of Jean Latour. Somewhere beyond that brown dike, those hundreds of black dots on the beach, somewhere behind the Hotel West End, straight as a bird flies, would be Jean Latour. It had meant so much, but now it was simply curiosity and pleasure that he felt: I am in a strange land.

His third-class compartment filled up slowly with workmen going home. It smelled of tobacco, corduroy, and sweat. They came in one by one, threw their bags on the shelf above, took out cigarette paper and rolled themselves cigarettes: blue blouses, blue eyes, shining golden faces. They didn't talk much except to whack a friend on the shoulder as they went past: 'Bonjour, vieux!' They observed Mark curiously out of the corners of their eyes. He felt too quick and too bright for these people. They didn't smile. In France, he thought, they would have smiled. Here they are silent. They sit and dream.

He had been looking inside the carriage and not out. Now he looked out. Now the flat land broke over his mind. He looked out and did not look away again. There it lay, Belgium: the flat green and gold fields (the wheat was early), the lines of trees going in every direction, the willows cut down to make round tufts. Two lines of poplars led off to the horizon like a great avenue. The train swerved and he saw that it was an avenue, a canal, lying as still as a mirror. In a field

The Hôtel du Rhin advertised itself with a small yellow sign. A painted hand pointed to the entrance. Mark followed a dark passage through a court and then into an anteroom full of leather armchairs. In a corner tables were already being laid for dinner. A woman was laying them. She stopped as he put down his bag and stood at the desk.

'Ah, Monsieur,' she said, bustling to take on her more formal personality of 'patronne.' 'You wish a room. For how long?' she asked. Mark decided that she must be a friend of the porter's. She had the same look in her eye.

'I don't know. Two weeks, perhaps. Not too expensive.' She wiped her hands on her apron and picked up his bag. 'Come along. Come and see.'

'I should like an attic room if I can — with some view of the sky.' He did not want to be buried somewhere in the dark of the court.

'Monsieur is an artist?' she asked, stopping at the fourth landing to catch her breath. 'Only an artist would ask for the sky. Voilà, Monsieur.' She opened a small dark room with a flourish.

Mark did not deny this. The room was ugly. The small window gave onto black roofs and a stretch of bare sky unadorned by a tree. The curtains were of some heavy brown material; the bed, under a dirty quilt, looked lumpy. But, Mark thought, It is just what I am looking for.

'How much?'

'Ten francs, Monsieur. And we bring you hot water every morning and whenever you ask for it.'

'All right.' It is exactly what I am looking for, he thought. 'But I shall need a table to write on.'

'We can arrange that, Monsieur. I'll just go and see what I have.' Mark was anxious to unpack, to go out and explore the city. A room becomes home, becomes 'one's own room,' when one has come back to it. Besides, he wanted to feel out its place in the city. He wanted to know what he was the centre of, what was going on around him, to be able to recognize the church bell that was just then ringing the hour, the rumble of the trains, the shrill sound of the tram-conductors' horns like children's whistles coming up to him from very far away. He wanted to create a pattern round him, a web of circumstance and fact and time (now he would go to a café and have an apéritif; now he would eat; now he would work.)

He decided not to wait any longer for the woman, and ran down the stairs and out without meeting her. The post-office was almost around the corner, very conveniently, and though there couldn't possibly be a letter from Jean Latour yet, there would be no harm in inquiring. He was amused, going into the gray dingy building, to observe the perfect nonchalance of the clerks. The Belgian post has none of the glamour of 'On His Majesty's Service.' Here no two clerks were dressed alike — some had on black aprons, some had on visors, almost all smoked as they worked. Handling the mail seemed to be a most casual business. Mark went up to a window marked 'Poste Restante.'

'Hé là! Jean, il y a quelqu'un à ton guichet!' But even when Jean had written the name down on a corner of paper and carried it somewhere in the back, where he slowly and laboriously lifted one letter after another and read the address, there was no letter. It had not been possible, of course, that there should be one. But Mark glimpsed the possibility of coming back here day after day asking the same question, and perhaps there never would be an answer. The small dark room became intolerable without the balance of this other adventure: one must come back to it from something besides a strange city. And at the same time, he thought, There will be an answer, I know. It would be too cruel — I can't have come all this way; I can't have been drawn here so strangely for *no* reason. There must be a reality at the other end.

Sometimes there was a nine o'clock mail and sometimes not. But, like all houses inhabited by sensitive people, the house of the Little Owls revolved around the mail man, 'le chéri.' Clairette waited for news from her sister in England, Annette from her cousins in the Ardennes, from her sister in Boulogne. She was adored by all the children and wrote to them regularly, letters full of drawings and jokes and advice and love.

Doro waited for news of any sort, though her actual correspondence was enormous, but she waited always for some unknown thing, 'the surprise' which when she was a child had often hidden in her father's pocket and now might so easily lie in the pocket of the 'chéri.'

The Little Owls were sitting, as so often at the end of the day, in the corner of Clairette's room. Claire smoked a cigarette and smiled over at them from the big chair. Of course they all heard Marthe's step on the stair. They all knew it was the evening mail, and they each disguised elaborately the thumping of her heart by all speaking at once.

'It is going to rain tomorrow,' said Annette.

'Where is Pascal?' asked Doro. Claire did not say anything, but pressed her cigarette out in the ash tray. All this took place in the flash of a second, a single often-repeated moment of suspense; for, well as they knew each other, they would not have admitted this childish impatience that seized them three times a day at the hour of the delivery of the mail. Marthe knocked.

'Come in.' They would not have admitted their impatience, but Marthe knew it perfectly well, and always put them out of their suspense as soon as possible by announcing exactly what there was.

'A letter for Madame from Ireland, none for Mamzelle, and one for Mamzelle from London.'

'From London! Who is it from, Doro?' asked Annette, looking over her shoulder. Claire had opened her letter and was reading it with the absent-minded smile of people reading letters. Doro looked at the envelope. It was typewritten. She tore it open.

'"Cher Monsieur" — But this is not for me,' she said, letting it fall in her hand.

'But of course it's for you — it's for Jean Latour. Have you forgotten who you are?'

'Yes, yes, I had forgotten.' Doro got up and walked to the window with the letter, reading it curiously. Who after all these years could be writing to Jean Latour? 'My dears, listen to this. It is an English boy who has read my poems — where did he ever find them? — and wants to come here to meet Monsieur Latour,' she said with her hands in her pockets. 'What am I to do?' She knew as she said it that what she would like to do would be to rush out and drop an express into the little boxes on the front of the trams so conveniently provided for these occasions. She would say: 'Come at once. Come tomorrow. How lovely that someone still cares for my poems, someone young!'

'Where is he?' asked Claire.

'In Ghent, my darling, in Ghent! Isn't it extraordinary?'

'Well, ask him to tea.'

'But he thinks I am a man.'

'Well, let him think so,' said Annette decidedly. 'Let him find out for himself. If he had eyes in his head he would have known you were a woman from the poems. As he didn't, let him find out for himself.'

'Clairette,' said Doro anxiously — for Claire was the one to whom they turned in any practical or worldly question — 'stop reading your letter and tell me what I am to do.'

'Well, write to him and tell him to come. It's quite simple. Much better not explain — what fun it will be — Oh, illustrious Monsieur Latour'; and their laughter was a bouquet, fresh and childlike, filling the room like a scent until Doro suddenly fled. The action was unprecedented.

'Incurable romantic,' said Annette, shaking her head. 'Toqué!' she added, tapping her forehead.

'No one is interested in my letter; it is too bad,' said Claire with mock sadness.

'We are all interested in ourselves, ma chère. Have you only just noticed that? I, for instance, am furious with my sister — I haven't heard for days. I am going to write to her.'

'Good night, Anne.'

'Good night. Sleep well. What emotions! We shall never hear the end of this,' she said. 'I am not going to like this English boy. He will smoke too much. The whole house will smell of smoke,' she said savagely.

'Oh, Annette, perhaps he is stupid and ugly, and probably he will only come once,' she said, smiling like a seraph, a seraph with a twinkle in his eye. 'Good night.' It was dear of Annette to be a little jealous of this chimera of an English boy.

Doro had fled into her room because in the middle of laughing she was overwhelmed with emotion at the idea of someone finding her poems after so many years. It seemed so extraordinary — though in the old days she had often received letters of this kind. But an English boy! And she was terrified at the idea of having to see him, of corresponding to some image he had of her in his mind — especially as he thought of her as a man. It would not matter, she thought, that I am not beautiful if I were a man, but I am afraid he will be horribly disappointed. It should be Clairette. Clairette is all that a poet should be, she thought, wringing her hands. And then she smiled at herself for attaching far too much importance to a letter such as anyone might write, such as she had so often written herself. She remembered (and remembering served to calm her agitation) how a French poet had written to congratulate her on her first book and added something about the verses being 'delicious, Monsieur, but just a little feminine.' How they had laughed over that 'Monsieur' in the blue room! Still smiling, she sat down at her desk and quickly took out a sheet of paper and a pen. She wrote quickly, inviting him to come to tea 'the day after tomorrow' at four-thirty. For just a second she hesitated over the signature, and then wrote firmly 'Jean Latour.' There, it was done.

Chapter Two

GEORGIA felt tired when she woke up. Sleep can be feathery or gold or lead: her sleep had been lead that night. She felt as if she had been devoured by it, as if it had lain inside her and weighed down every vein and artery with lead. She had not dreamed. She had lain weighed down by sleep, and now she opened her eyes as the breakfast trays were brought in.

'Thank you, Alice. Don't pull the curtains. My eyes are tired. Darling, wake up.'

Manuele hated waking up. He groaned as she leaned over to kiss him. 'Wake up, darling. Here's your breakfast.' When he woke up, he woke up suddenly and completely and leaped out of bed. 'Oh, Manuele, you're much too energetic,' she said, sitting up sleepily. He came back smelling of toothpaste and rubbed his prickly chin against hers. 'Don't, you brute, don't rub me the wrong way. You feel like a gooseberry.' He laid her tray on her lap and then got back into bed and disappeared behind the paper.

'How you can read the paper before you've had your coffee I don't know,' said Georgia, picking up the letters one by one from her tray. Two bills, a letter from her aunt in Italy, a letter postmarked Ghent. She turned it over in her hand, weighed it, a fat letter. She did not want to open it yet. The room felt heavy with sleep, with her tiredness; it smelled of sleep. She did not want to be woken up or to have to feel just yet. She poured out her coffee and drank half a cup quickly. But she would have to open it; the letter was there, a locked door. Behind it might lie a spot of blood, a corpse. It was too silly to lie here thinking what might be in the letter and not to open it. She did not want to be upset. She did not, this morning, want to be loved too much. And she had a premonition, glancing over at Manuele, who was trying to eat and read at the same time, she had a premonition that this would not be an easy letter to read unmoved. Still looking at him she tore it open, her fingers performing the mechanical gesture as if they held nothing unusual. At the top it said 'On board the *Prince Leopold.*'

'The Germans are massing troops on the Austrian frontier,' said Manuele suddenly. (My darling, until this moment there has been too much to do and I have managed not to realize that I shan't see you again.) 'Georgia, did you hear what I said? It looks serious,' he went on persistently.

'Yes, darling, how dreadful! But they have done that before, after all.' (Now I do realize it, now that already there is a mile or so of water between us, already a limbo, and I cannot quite remember your face, now I know how much I miss you. You must believe that it is something like bleeding, bleeding horribly from a wound.)

'How callous you are, Georgia! Here we are on the brink of war, and you just go on reading your letters and not listening to me.'

'I'm sorry, darling. I'm listening.' She let the letter fall in her hand. (But this is not what I want. I don't want him to suffer.)

'What is the matter with you, Georgia? You look quite white.'

'I slept badly.'

'You slept like a rock.'

'I know, but it was a bad kind of sleep, exhausting.' Oh, God, let him go back to his paper. This is unendurable. (Or having been bruised with the hose the Nazis are fond of using, which leaves no mark. I know that I have no right to write to you like this. My place in your life is a *divertissement*, and when it ceases to be that it will be no good to you.) This is a terrible letter. He shouldn't have written it. It's not fair.

'Well, take it easy today. Let's do something quiet — let's go to Richmond and go out in a boat, or to the zoo,' said Manuele, stroking the inside of her elbow.

No, I can't stand this. Oh let me be alone for half an hour. Don't touch me. 'Yes, darling, that's a good idea. Now let me finish my letters in peace, *please*.' The first part of the sentence she had managed very nicely, but just at the end her voice shot out with misery and impatience.

'All right, femme hystérique. I'll be quiet,' he said, and went mercifully back to the paper.

(The trouble is that one is torn between wanting to make things important and accepting them as they are. You have never said you loved me. Suddenly I remember that you have never said it. You do not love me, then. But you have allowed me to love you too much; you have set me alight like a bonfire, and now leave me to find my own way of putting it out. My darling, you are quite right, it is I who am leaving, not you. But you will admit that you are glad I have gone, that you are relieved.) He's right. I don't love him. I love him, but not in the way he wants to be loved. I love him in such a different way, with all my capacity for delight. But why does one always want the other kind, why must one want the power to make people suffer? Oh, my darling child. I'm going to cry. I'm going to cry.

'The new Priestley play sounds pretty poor — too bad for Polly.'

I'm going to cry. 'What's wrong with you, Georgia? You look as if you had seen a ghost.'

'Nothing, nothing.' Her voice found the clear high pitch tears hide themselves in. Manuele, the most sensitive person in the world, could be as blind as this sometimes — luckily. The idea that he might turn and ask to see the letter, or that he might guess, stopped the tears like a spell. Anything but that.

'I'm getting up.' She fled into the bathroom, into the loud safe noise of water running, and there she sat and finished the letter which she did not want to finish, for what am I going to do now? How am I going to answer? How easily you have taken this joy, she thought, slipping into the warm water and lying there.

Some people are inspired in their baths, come to great decisions, write poems, find mathematical formulas in their baths. But Georgia never thought of anything in her bath. She let herself taste the luxury of being simply light and warm, with nothing to be done and no decision to make. So today it was only shivering on the carpet that she went on thinking, How easily you have taken this joy, how arrogantly. But he will get over it, she added. He's young. He has work to do. In spite of the intensity of this moment he will get over it. Perhaps he is already over it, she thought, drying her toes.

In Ghent, Mark was shaving. He had looked out of the window into the square of sky and saw that it was gray, a gray, glaring sky without charm. Today Georgia gets my letter; perhaps she is reading it now. Letters are terrible in their finality, in the fact that when they arrive they are already the past masquerading as the present, thrown in under the door, falling on the carpet as if they had just blown in fresh from the pen, whereas in reality they are dead. My letter, he thought, is a disgrace. She will be hurt. She will be worried. I have behaved like a blundering schoolboy.

But it is not the mind that makes one behave like this, nor even the heart that is young and patient and wary and infinitely vulnerable. Neither one would write such a wrong letter. It is a letter written in blood. For Georgia is in me now like a poison. All that rot about knowledge is just rot compared with the remembered kiss, with the ache for one thing only. An inessential thing, not the thing in the end that I most want, but a secret poison that has me now.

He had finished shaving. He turned to the bed, crumpled sheets, the breakfast tray with its crumbs, its half-eaten jam, its cup with a brown sediment at the bottom. He looked once round the dingy walls and out at the piece of sky. This might be hell or it might be the one thing in the world he had asked. This morning he would work. He would not go out for the post until lunch time. He would protect himself from the waste of disillusion, the violence of waiting and being disappointed, and he would work.

The minute he sat down at the table for the first time since he had arrived, and opened the blue envelope with the sheets of manuscript, and set out his pen and pencil and the old piece of red blotting paper, he felt released. This, after all, he said to himself, is my life. All the rest doesn't matter — even Georgia, even the line of her chin is nothing to this passion: to sit alone in a strange city and talk to oneself, set one word down after another until suddenly the meaning is evident, the thing is there — the small truth of the morning set out before me.

Manuele knocked at the door. 'I want to shave.'

'Come along, come along. I'm just drying myself, but I think you can squeeze in.'

'Good morning, savage creature.' He took her two hands and looked at her. 'All right?'

'All right.'

'Even though the European war will burst on us at any minute?' She nodded. She nodded, and went out with the letter hidden under her nightgown. I have told Manuele that it is all right, she thought. And by some miracle it was all right. I shall write him a letter. I shall write to him, and by tomorrow there will be a different answer. He will be all right. After all, he has always known — Manuele, he has known about Manuele. He has seen how my roots are here. There is nothing to be done about it. He has betrayed nothing. It is easy for him; a single painful moment and it is over. But I have betrayed myself. I have allowed a hot summer day and a thunderstorm, I have allowed tenderness and the sudden power of a hand in love with its moment of lightning, to threaten a thing built up slowly out of years. I have allowed the deepest thing in my life to be swept away on a tide of emotion. I have been betrayed; but Manuele, Manuele, my husband, who will never know, who will never guess, I have not betrayed you. I have only given you one more triumph. I have only added one more tower to the citadel of our love.

Now I shall get dressed, she thought. And I will begin the landscape I have had in my mind. It is a gray day, a good day for work. And then I shall write to Mark, very simply and quietly, and he will surely understand.

So it is possible, if one must, to make the most complicated things simple. It is possible for the spirit at the moment of decision to soar out, to arrive apparently without effort at the peak, to survey a situation complete like a landscape from the top of a mountain. In the exhilaration of the peak one forgets that one must still find the way down, that it is not the peaks that are difficult to negotiate but the long slow gray descents to the plain, that it is not life at its points of emergency, terror, or despair that is terrible but life at its simplest and most ordinary.

For the moment Georgia had found the peak. For the moment Mark across the channel had found it. Temporary security of this kind is precious. Each silently and alone used it, set it down in paint, in words.

Chapter Three

ONCE Mark had received the little note in the round clear handwriting inviting him to tea, he felt extraordinarily peaceful. The suspense had gone before. Now he waited patiently for the hour. Early in the afternoon he went to the 'Parc' with Jean Latour in his pocket. He went in among the formal parterres, this too-formal garden, looking for a place where he could lie down in the grass. But it all looked like a carpet one would not dare tread on. Finally he came to a little grove of beech trees: long green trunks lifted straight up to an incredible height, and bursting into sprays of transparent lime-colored leaves, the earth carpeted with copper from the autumn before, the sun falling in patches. He sat down under a tree. Now it will happen or it won't, he thought, his hand in his pocket touching the smooth cover of the book. There is nothing further to be done. He read here and there, saying the words that had become so familiar that he no longer listened to their sense but only to their sound. Sitting under the tree he felt as if flowers were falling on his head, as if the sun were flowers. Sometimes one has a feeling of festival for no reason: it is as if everything on earth were celebrating something. Perhaps after all — it is for me that all this sings and shines today, for I am meeting Jean Latour, he thought.

In the kitchen on the Chaussée de Courtrai Doro was calming her nerves by arranging the tray for tea, a tiny glass vase with three Chinese pinks in it, a dish of strawberries she had just been picking in the garden. By a miracle there was sun, she thought, remembering the dank atmosphere of the day before. Once more the contrast between how she felt (for she felt absurdly young and frightened) and how she looked swept over her as she cut the raisin bread into thin slices. Marthe looked on, and kept up a steady stream of conversation.

'Mamzelle Le Coq told me that Mamzelle is expecting an English gentleman.'

'Yes, Marthe, an admirer,' said Doro, laughing suddenly, as she could, as if it were a bubble breaking lightly inside her.

'Ah, Mamzelle, no one but Mamzelle can cut such fine slices of bread — you have the hands of an angel.'

'A poor old angel, Marthe,' said Doro, looking down at her tiny hands. 'What time is it?' she asked suddenly.

'Just a quarter past four, Mamzelle.' (A quarter of an hour, and she would have to face this stranger who expected so much of her.)

'Bring the tray up a few minutes after he arrives.' (Tea would be a means of getting over the first few moments.)

'Yes, Mamzelle. Just as you say.' Doro slipped through the swinging door like a shadow. She had been there a moment before, and now she was gone.

Mark turned into the Chaussée looking up at the

forbidding houses, ugly houses, most of them, built since the war. Cold stone faces with horrible lace curtains at the windows. Somewhere along here he had been told at the hotel he would see a red-brick house with 'Cours d'Education' on it. Yes, there across the street was — not the great formal building he had expected, but a little low house surrounded with a box hedge and with a tiny garden in front of it. Many wide windows. It looked simply like a house, a house someone might have invented for himself. It was curious to think of Jean Latour as a schoolmaster, but because the school did not look like a school it was encouraging. He glanced up at the windows on the second floor imagining that he saw a gray head looking out between the curtains, but of course he imagined it. He went up the path between two beds of Chinese pinks and rang the bell. The longest moment is always the moment between ringing a bell and being let in. It is a continent to cross, the sill which divides the beggar from the guest, the stranger from the friend. Marthe opened the door with the peculiar eagerness and excitement she brought to all her tasks, and smiled at him warmly, saying before he had a chance to speak:

'Oh, Mamzelle is expecting you, Monsieur. Will you follow me?' He stopped on the landing and looked down at the green plot of grass and the cherry tree, wondering if he were going to have to face a maiden sister before being introduced to the poet himself. Marthe knocked at the door.

'Come in.' With every sense alert Mark noticed at once the timbre of the voice, tired and soft and fibrous all at once. Then he was in the room. He had an impression of being too big for it, and of there being a great deal of light reflected from many small objects, of many colors, and then he saw the small figure before him.

'You are Jean Latour,' he said, almost before he knew himself what he was saying. But it was unmistakable. Of course she was, that blue bow at her throat, the great gray eyes (she was holding her glasses in her left hand as she held out her right). How could he have been so stupid as not to know at once — of course Jean Latour was a woman; of course this woman was Jean Latour.

The minute he said 'You are Jean Latour' with such perfect conviction, as if he had always known she would look exactly like that, she knew that it would be all right. But she was startled, almost as startled as he had been; there was something in his look as he stood there that reminded her of someone. It was as if she had seen him before — the tall figure with hands hanging loosely at his sides and the very dark eyes. Who was it he looked like?

'Sit down. Sit on the corner of the sofa where you can look into the garden, and I'll sit here,' she said, pulling the little armchair up so that she could see his face.

'You are Jean Latour,' he said again, thinking he had never seen such a strange and wonderful face.

'Tea will be here in a moment,' she said, irrelevantly thinking, it is the Watteau Gilles, of course. It is unmistakable. 'How long have you been in Ghent?'

'Just two days.'

'And how long do you plan to stay?'

'I don't know.' These are the preliminaries. They have to be got through to allow the eye and the ear time to reconnoitre. They sat rather stiffly, Mark on the high sofa, Doro opposite him leaning forward on her elbow.

'Don't put on your glasses,' he said suddenly, as she lifted them mechanically to shut out the light.

'But I can't see properly without them. You are working here?' She did not put on her glasses.

'Yes.' We have had enough of this. It is time to plunge in, he thought. 'But you know I came to Belgium to find you.' There, it was said. Now it was said he felt he must embroider the sentence. He must give her time to bridge quietly and at her ease the distance between their impersonal meeting and this absolutely personal statement, this absolutely personal relationship on which they must embark. 'Yes, I crossed the channel and borrowed the money to come here for only one reason — to find you.'

'Why?' asked Doro simply. When such extraordinary things happen one can only take them simply.

'Because I don't know anyone I can talk to.'

'You speak French very well for an Englishman.'

'I'm not English. I'm half French. My father was a French Jew. My mother was American.'

'Oh.' For the first time a silence fell between them. Mark looked out of the window. Doro watched him. She thought, in repose his face looks strained, the minute he speaks it lights up as if a lamp were lighted. It becomes transparent. Seeing him speak, I thought, 'What a charming boy!' Seeing him silent there is more, and the more is something stern and something self-defeated.

'What a lovely garden! Are there strawberries?' he said. It was almost the garden he had invented as a child, a plum tree and a cherry tree; but there must be a strawberry bed. Everything here looked as if he had seen it before somewhere, or dreamed it and forgotten the dream until he saw it.

'Not only have we a strawberry bed, but look' — Marthe was just bringing in the tray — 'Here are the strawberries I picked this afternoon. By a miracle we have strawberries in April this year. Here on the little table, Marthe.'

Mark had come to talk, but now he did not want to talk. He just wanted to sit here forever and watch the small deft hands pouring tea out of the pot, lifting the cover to look into it.

'Marthe will never make it strong enough.' She stirred it with a spoon.

'Do you live here alone?'

'Oh, no. I live with two friends, two old ladies like myself. You must see them next time you come'; for it was taken for granted already that he would come again.

'And you have a school?'

'Yes. You have come so far expecting to find a poet and you have found a school-teacher.'

'I was afraid you would turn out to be a fat old man, a minister of agriculture or something — and now you're — you're ——'

'An old maid,' she laughed. He had not heard her laugh before. For some reason it brought tears to his eyes.

'I have been looking for you all my life.' He realized

that with her for the first time in his life he could speak the truth. She did not quickly deny it. She listened and accepted. Like her poems, she was transparent. She could accept the truth. She could accept the heart.

'It is a long time since anyone has spoken of my poems — anyone young,' she said softly.

'You'll read them to me?'

'Yes, if you like' — she made a little deprecatory gesture. 'They are nothing, you know. They are like sketches for a poem I never wrote.'

'I was living alone in a little town in England. A friend lent me his house. One night it rained.' (In speaking French Mark found himself choosing his words carefully. In speaking to her they fell into a pattern. He noticed this at once.) 'I went walking about like a cat, feeling so dull I didn't know what to do with myself, and quite by accident I pulled your "Poèmes, 1903" out of the shelf. I read it right through, and all night lines kept running through my head. You see, I feel sure that you are after the same thing I am. I have been so lonely,' he said simply. 'I have felt so ashamed of myself in this age of great causes. I have a friend who has gone to Spain. And then to find you, affirming everything I believe for myself, making it seem possible, right. I couldn't believe there was someone like me, a man' — he smiled; — they smiled together, embarked on the end of the sentence together — 'who wanted transparency more than anything. And I thought I must come and find you, because here at last was someone I could talk to.'

They sat and looked out into the garden. When one finally arrives at the end of a long journey there is nothing to say. There is everything to say and everything can wait. Doro felt an overwhelming sense of peace and gratitude, that at last and in her lifetime her poems had reached the person for whom they were written.

'You are not drinking your tea.'

'Neither are you.'

They looked down and smiled, each smiling alone, smiling together. Mark had suffered so long from social conventions, from living in an artificial atmosphere — even with Georgia there was the artificiality, the terrible consciousness and reserve of a physical element that turned every word into a symbol for something else. If life had a pattern, part of its pattern was surely that he should meet this woman when their relationship could be absolutely direct and shorn of any temporal conflict. He could not yet believe that here in this room he could be silent when he wanted to, could speak when he wanted to and say anything; and that because the essence of their relationship must be spiritual, having to do, he saw now, with a way of life as well as a personality, it might be the answer to all personal despair: it might achieve for him what the embracing of communism had done for Al.

'You must begin at the beginning and tell me where you were born and everything that has happened to you since, what cities you have lived in, how it is that you speak French so well, how it is,' she said, looking at him for the first time (she had been speaking turning the cup in the saucer with one hand and looking down), 'how it is that you are lonely.'

He began at the beginning and described his life.

She watched his face, learning more from it, from the hesitation in the speech, from the sudden frown, from the quick nervous gesture across his forehead as if he were casting something away, than from the words. She learned more from his hands, small for a man, and strong, with curious very oval nails, from his characteristic gesture of suddenly pulling his hair in exasperation or pleasure, than from anything he said.

As Mark talked he felt as if he were a child drawing a house in crayon with a garden. Everything that had happened to him so far seemed incredibly simple, and now that it was finished, so unimportant compared to the effort of telling it with all its implications to someone who could understand. But he did not speak of Georgia. He felt shy about it, though he knew he was wrong to be shy. But looking at that pure, stern face of which the eyes never wavered, he did not know quite how to tell it. He felt that it had some relation to his being here now, and that that was something he could not explain yet because he did not know it himself.

'There is a great deal that you have not told me — but there is time,' she said when he had finished. 'Come, I want to show you the room where I work. You must get to know the whole house.' She led the way through the narrow passage. Seeing the great desk in the middle with its piles of notebooks, its rows of pencils, Mark was moved. He stood at it a moment without speaking.

'But you are still writing?'

'No,' she said softly. 'Now it is your turn to write. Mine is finished.'

'Why? Why? It's just now that you should write.'

'I wonder. I think perhaps it is more important that I should teach now — and besides, you know, I must earn my living,' she said, with one hand in her pocket and a certain pride.

'But it is just now that you must have everything to say. I have this feeling, that everything I'm doing is simply an exercise, a discipline, a training so that when I really have something to say I shall be able to go straight to it. Young, one knows nothing; one can only guess; one can only *feel*,' he added contemptuously.

'And you think one does more than that when one is old? The only thing I see clearly and really long to write about is my childhood; isn't it strange?' Mark had sat down in the chair at the desk. She brought out a child's armchair with a bright red cushion from under the desk. 'This is where my children sit when there is a very difficult lesson, and you know, it is a little like Aladdin's carpet. It is remarkable how quickly they learn in this chair.' She was sitting in it now, so tiny that it seemed to have been built for her. 'What I am longing to have time to write,' she said, 'is the smell of the old house where I went to school — in Mons — with its walls paneled in damask, one cherry color and the other yellow, where our inkstained desks almost touched the great gilt mirrors, reflecting as if in water twenty little girls with bows in their hair. At recess I used to run away with "David Copperfield" or Victor Hugo in my pocket and hide under a lilac bush, giving up at once my whole life to this other life, to become nothing but delight and tears over an imaginary little boy. That is what I want to write — after these sixty-three years of life all I can find to write about. And it is nothing more,' she said, getting up and going to the window, 'than the syllable a bird might utter before going to sleep — you see.'

Hearing her speak, Mark felt as if he had fallen under a spell. He had never heard French so beautifully, so justly spoken. He wished he could remember each word, the very gracious shape of the sentences. After she had finished he went on listening in silence. And then he said:

'I wonder if that is because everything has been sifted out. What is *there*, what you remember, is as perfect as a leaf in a Chinese painting. There are spaces around it — is it only time that can set the proper spaces around experience?' he asked.

'I don't know. I don't know. You mustn't expect me to be able to answer such questions,' she said, smiling at him; she felt very tired. 'Come; come into the garden before you go.' They went out onto the landing and down the stairs. For the first time this year the white table, the bench, and the white armchair had been put out under the cherry tree. Doro stopped on the stairs. 'Look. This is my favorite place in the house. I love to stop and look down at the cherry tree and the table and chairs. I have often thought how strangely they sum up our three lives, joined and set apart — their silence, their solitary intimacy. But I forget, I forget that we have only known each other half an hour. And you have not met the others.' They went out through the dining-room door.

'That,' she said, pointing with a large gesture to a black bed at their feet, 'is the rose-bed.' It was hedged in with a border of Chinese pinks. They walked slowly down the little cinder path, and it seemed to Mark that this was a journey around the world, and that in the rose-bed and the gooseberry-bed which they were just reaching he would see Italy and Ireland, and even a country that no one had yet discovered. Because of the fruit trees making umbrellas of shade here and there the garden seemed much bigger than it was. They came out suddenly into the light and were confronted with a barrage of gooseberries, a plot of grass, and before the sight, the *smell* of strawberries in a warm wave.

'Oh, there are the strawberries.'

'Yes, a perfect jungle of them.' Mark was already on his knees. 'Who's this?' As he stooped over he saw a small, inquisitive face look out at him.

'That's Pascal.' Pascal wagged his tail and yawned as if to say, It is a bore that people always have to come and interrupt me just as I have achieved a certain detachment from the world.

Mark laughed as he got up. 'He's evidently a very superior person. Have a strawberry?'

'Thanks.' They walked slowly up again toward the house. Again Mark, adjusting his steps to her small ones, felt that he was a giant. His head touched the branches of the cherry, and he had to stoop as he walked under it.

'Do you read English? Could you read my poem, do you think?'

'A little — I think I could guess your poem — but you must read it to me and translate. The day after tomorrow.' It had been on the tip of her tongue to say 'tomorrow,' but even joy can strain the heart, and she wanted time to taste this slowly. So she said: 'The day after tomorrow. Come to lunch. Then you will meet the Little Owls.' They had been so deep in conversation they had not noticed that Annette and Claire were having their tea already.

'He has a nice face,' said Clairette.

'But he doesn't look English at all,' said Annette, standing up to get a better view. Just then Doro pushed open the door, with a little gasp at finding them there.

'Well,' she said, 'here he is! Come in, Mark, and have a second cup! This is Mark Taylor, Mademoiselle Le Coq, Madame Mentel.'

For the first time since he had come into this house Mark felt shy. He bowed, and sat down in the chair Doro offered him. He took out a package of cigarettes, offered one first to Doro, who shook her head, then to Annette, who looked quite startled, and finally to Clairette, who smiled. (She is very beautiful, he thought, but I like Jean Latour's face better.)

'Thank you. It's a luxury to have an English cigarette. I'll smoke it after tea.'

'You must know, Mark,' said Doro, who was thinking how differently one sees a person when he is with others as if on a stage, 'that it is a very great occasion when Clairette smokes a cigarette at tea.'

'It is a great occasion,' he said solemnly. 'If you knew,' he said, turning to Annette, 'how happy I am to be here it would be contagious.'

'You flatter us, my boy.' And then they all laughed, out of relief, out of nervousness, out of the need to laugh a little together.

'You know, I can only call you Monsieur,' said Mark to Doro. 'I don't yet know your name. I think I had better know it' — for he thought he would have to write her a letter when he got home. It was curious how one often wanted to escape people in order to be able to write to them.

'My name is Dorothée, Dorothée Latour, but I am really Doro, and that is Clairette and that is Anne. I think Mark is a Little Owl already, he has such black hair.'

'Of course he is a Little Owl.' Annette had been watching him, and it was the way he spread jam on his bread and butter that convinced her of this. 'Look, he is almost as fantastic as I am with his layers of jam!'

Mark looked down at the piece of bread he had covered with a thick red layer. He had not done that since he was a child in the kitchen at Nice, when Annie used to let him have bread and butter and jam in the middle of the morning.

'Oh.'

'Go right ahead,' said Doro, smiling. 'We've teased Annette so much that she is delighted to have a victim.' How happy she felt to have him eat in her house, to have him here completing the fourth side of the table.

Mark was sitting opposite Claire. He observed her as he ate and drank; for whenever he was nervous he ate a great deal, and now he was starting on a second piece of bread. He liked her more and more.

'You are also a writer?' he asked.

'Now and then.'

'Yes, Mark, you must read her stories. You will like them.' Sitting there between these three old ladies whose lives lay behind him, Mark felt suddenly ashamed and shy and sad.

'But you are a poet,' said Clairette kindly.

'You see, we know all about you,' Annette passed him the jam again. 'What! No more jam? Ah! These poets, they live on words,' she laughed. 'What! Only two slices of bread thickly covered with jam? There is the whole jar waiting for you!'

'You'll make him choke,' said Doro, laughing. Just at that moment he did choke. Annette whacked him hard on the back.

'I'm afraid the cure will kill,' said Claire quietly.

Mark was purple. It was extraordinary how uncomfortable a crumb could make one feel.

'Come along. Come upstairs and get a glass of water.' Doro wanted quickly to get him away. He followed her, waving a hand at the Little Owls. Five minutes later he knocked at Doro's door. She was sitting at the window, back to him.

'All right again?'

'Yes, thanks.' The minute he stepped back into her room he felt that it was a private world. It was good to have been taken out of it for a little while to have this sense of coming home now. 'Hadn't we better go down?' he asked anxiously.

'No,' she said. 'Come and sit down a minute before you go.' Now that they had been away and come back, it was as if something had been established in the temporary absence, as if perhaps some part of them each had stayed in this room and they had come back to find it there. Looking at her now, Mark thought he had never seen such eyes. They were so big that they seemed to be her whole face, her whole self. It was like looking at an infinity which could stoop to cherish.

But always one must leave; always one must get up and go away; one must go back to one's own solitude; one must find one's own silence.

'I must go,' he said. They walked to the door arm in arm.

'Don't come down. I can find my way out. But shouldn't I say good-bye to them?' But he wanted to go without saying good-bye, to go garlanded, to go wreathed as he was in a silence.

'No, no. I'll say good-bye for you. I'm afraid they are already upstairs in their rooms.' Then he was gone.

Doro sat in the armchair with the tea tray in front of her and ate the strawberries one by one that they had forgotten, as if in the sweet sour taste she were eating the spring, she were somehow assimilating the spring that had come to her. I suppose she thought: This is why one is a poet, so that some day, sooner or later, one can say the right thing to the right person at the right time. That Mark should look like the Gilles, that he should have found her across all these years, seemed in no way extraordinary now that it had happened. Yesterday it would have been impossible. One does not hope for such things: they happen. She wondered what it was that he had not told her, that lay behind his face as he talked like a shadow, and she wondered if she would be able to help.

Out on the street Mark felt only a desire to run, to shout, to stop an old lady who was passing him with such a sour expression, to take her in his arms and say, 'Oh, if you only knew, if you only knew how good life is, how incredibly, impossibly good it is!' He was smiling as he walked. He felt that he was like a sun walking down the street. People turned to look at him. He felt full of light. He felt hungry. He stopped at a café to order a beer and a paper and pen. He must write and thank her at once. He must sing. He must send her some flowers.

He sat drinking his beer and thinking. He thought of Georgia. But that is different, he thought. Here with Jean Latour I am finding myself; it's almost as if she were myself. With Georgia I am trying to possess, to understand, to share something that is not myself, that is miles away from myself. I am trying to bridge an abyss, as love does. But this is not love. It is revelation, he thought; it is transparency.

He wrote a short note sending her his address, which he had forgotten to give her, and paid for his beer. Now he would look for a florist. He would have to go into the centre of town for that. He hopped onto a tram as it was moving, with the ease that joy gives to everything. He felt that today he could not make a wrong move, he could not stumble.

It seemed a long way, past quays and canals lined with trees, over bridges until he saw St. Bavon, the square, graceful tower, and jumped off, partly because he wanted suddenly to see something of Ghent. He thought he would go in and look at the Van Eyck 'Adoration of the Lamb.' He had been living such a curious life of his own, he felt suddenly as if the shutter of his mind were opened and he could look out. Here he was in Ghent, the city of flowers, of fine linen, of wars, and wheat coming up still canals in great barges.

He was at the centre of a whole world to be explored.

But first he must find flowers. Van Eyck could wait, would be there forever but this moment in his life would never happen again. He stood in the street not knowing which way to go. A gendarme stopped to ask him, 'Can I direct you, Monsieur?'

'What? What? Oh, yes. Can you direct me to a florist?' You do not understand, he thought, that I must send flowers, that I cannot wait another minute.

'Just over to the left, Monsieur.'

'Thank you.' The glass window full of floral wreaths and bunches of roses looked forbidding. A fat woman in felt slippers padded in as the bell jangled.

'Have you any lilies of the valley? And forget-me-nots?' he asked.

'Yes, right here, Monsieur.'

'Good.' He thought he had never liked his own name so well as when he wrote 'Mark' on the card and slipped it into an envelope.

Chapter Four

WHEN Mark woke up the next morning he lay in bed waiting for his breakfast and looking at the little square of blue he could see from his bed. At night there were two stars, in the morning this piece of sky that told everything about the day and the night. He lay thinking that by all means this day should be distinguished. Now there was no excuse for poor work, for misery, for laziness. He would work all morning and then go for the mail. Mark always thought, glibly, that he would work all morning; the phrase was easy to say. It might appear in any German-English grammar with such sentences as 'Is your grandmother living?' and 'Where is the key to the house?' So one might say, 'Have you been working all morning?' At twelve o'clock Mark could answer in the affirmative. But it would be difficult to describe the variety of experience implied in the answer.

First there had been the moment after breakfast when the room looked unspeakably sordid. Every instinct told him to go out for a walk and come back when it was made up, but the wary creature who made him write was firm about this. If he went out, a thousand impressions on the street would confuse the clear images of the night. The creature had discovered this long ago, and now made use of it mercilessly. He must sit down while his cigarette was still half smoked; he must sit down and face the empty white sheet of paper. This was the daily nightmare. There was a moment always when it would seem better to write anything, a remembered poem, half of 'Alice in Wonderland' on it, anything to escape the intolerable blank before him. Every morning at this moment it was evident that he could not write, that everything he had done so far was an accident, a mistake, that he had been suffering from some delusion. Meanwhile he had taken out the sheaf which contained the poem up to now. The temptation was to begin at the beginning and read it through in order to get himself started, but he had done this so often already that instead of starting a train of thought it simply put him to sleep. He must glance hastily over the last three stanzas. He must sharpen three pencils. He must get up and walk up and down; he must come back to write a single phrase at the top of the page, he must sit down with his head in his hands for a minute, not thinking of it, thinking of anything *but* it. The creative mind is a donkey. Beat it, hold a carrot in front of its nose, still it may refuse to budge. Every single morning as far back as he could remember a prolonged struggle took place until very slowly, almost imperceptibly, the donkey would take one step, then two, and finally get away at a brisk trot. When a single stanza was completed the floor around him would be littered with sheets of paper. Then he would read it aloud and decide as he heard it that it was really good, the best I've done, a blessed state never lasting more than a few minutes. It was followed by despair and sudden tiredness. It is unutterably bad, he would think, smoke a cigarette, and begin again, for now the donkey was trotting it was like automatic movement. The difficulty was to stop.

At twelve Mark had typed out what he had done that morning. At this point he felt simply like any laborer who has set a chimney on a house or painted a door. Neither good nor bad, it was simply done. He was free of it. He could go out and see if there was any mail.

There was a different man at the window this morning when he asked for letters. It was necessary to spell out his name once more and watch the black alpaca back disappear slowly into the cavern in the rear, watch the man shake his head as if the name Mark Taylor were scarcely credible, and shuffle incompetently through a pack of letters. He returned equally slowly with a small white envelope. Mark recognized the childish irregular writing at once: Georgia.

He looked at it a second and then put it in his pocket. Where to go, how to read it? He felt that he must be somewhere where he could not be seen, where his face need not be a mask, that to read this letter where he could be observed would be like standing naked in the street. He went out, down the narrow street, and into the square in front of the station. He jumped onto a tram. People on trams he thought are looking out, not in. Here I am safe. He got into a first-class compartment; there was no one there but a very old lady. At such a moment there is comfort in the old. It would not matter to her what the young man opposite was thinking. Now.

Already he wondered at how thin it was, one page, he thought, tearing open the envelope. The conductor was standing just over him. Mark fumbled in his pocket, reading at the same time. He brought out a franc and handed it to the conductor.

(Darling, I have been wandering about the house doing the flowers and ordering the dinner with your letter in my pocket, wondering how to answer it. All this has happened so quickly, like a beautiful thunderstorm. I don't know yet what life will look like when it clears away. You are a wild, sweet extravagance which I think my heart can't quite afford. Mark, darling, can you understand that I do love you in the simplest way, and truly, but I think you must not let it seize your whole life and it must stay outside of mine.)

Mark looked up and saw that the conductor was still standing there watching him, waiting for something.

'Well?' said Mark, with rage in his voice. The old lady turned and stared.

'Another fifteen centimes, Monsieur. I did not want to interrupt Monsieur,' the conductor leered. Mark put fifty centimes into his hand and got up. He walked down the middle of the rocking tram onto the platform. The conductor pursued him with the change.

'Your change.' He gave Mark an angry look, and Mark thought he would gladly punch him in the face. Here in the trolley car he was filled with such anger against this innocent man who was just then blowing his ridiculous brass horn to announce an 'Arrêt,' he was so angry that he would have liked to go up and insult him on purpose to get into a fight. Anything not to have to read again or think of the letter.

He jumped carelessly off the tram at the next stop and twisted his ankle; his marvellous equilibrium of yesterday had left him completely. But it did not matter. It was almost a relief to be bothered with something outside, to be absorbed for a moment in rubbing it and sitting down on a bench like anyone else, like anyone of the people passing on their way to shop or to visit an aunt. The tram had stopped by a canal, flanked with cold, shuttered houses, a line of maples making it look secret and dark. Here Mark found a bench. He pulled out the letter and read it again, weighing each word, measuring the power of each as if there were a huge thought to be discovered behind them, as if they were a secret language with a key, whereas he knew perfectly well that in writing them Georgia had not measured them; any conclusions he might reach would be false, magnified and blurred like a stone through water.

The momentary rage he had felt on reading the letter had spent itself on the tram-conductor. He was not angry with Georgia now. He was not angry with her for confusing him with a letter full of half-words, full of implications which there is just no way for me to understand or accept, he thought bitterly. It is just when one is in love, when one is in this highly aware state, when every word, every gesture seems to be full of meaning, to bear the infinite possibility in it, that one wants clarity, that one wants to be told things in simple sentences. This is the necessity that drives people to ask over and over again at different times of the day and night, 'Do you love me?' because they are in a state of such perpetual suspense and uncertainty that they must be constantly reassured. But Georgia is trying to say that she does not love me; how infinitely more complex and difficult, needing more than three words, for I must know exactly how she does and how she does not love me. Of course there is Manuele. There always was Manuele. There was Manuele when she came to Carter's flat.

Mark was now walking along the canal. His ankle had stopped hurting, and now he had to admit the growing pain in his mind, driving him to walk faster and faster, incongruous, erratic, out of tempo with these dead waters, these rows of old houses — 'Quai du Compromis.' Who or what was compromised here, he wondered. He crossed a bridge as the houses shut off the road to go down right to the water's edge, leaning a little as if in a moment the whole row might disappear soundlessly with hardly a splash. He was passing big formal buildings now — a hospital?

No word that Jean Latour would say could substitute, he thought, for this hunger planted in his breast, devouring him like a fever. Looking back to the day before it seemed centuries ago, like the world of one's childhood when everything becomes quite simple in retrospect; one remembers it tenderly, believing there were no difficulties then and one was safe.

Yesterday he had been safe. He had been enclosed in a peaceful, unreal world, he thought. And there was no solution. None. The canal turned. He stood a moment on the wide bridge looking down at the brown still water. There is no way to stop this ache except to die, he thought. As long as you live you will still hunger and thirst. You might as well admit it now. Standing on the bridge and looking down (it trembled as a trolley crashed over it), Mark wondered what he would do.

He had never thought of the future. It is absurd, he decided; I imagined this would go on forever. I have been thinking that it was just beginning and already it is ended. This is the way things end, then, for no reason. They are suddenly cut down like flowers, the heart cut down like a flower. But you can't do this to me, he said, turning away from the bridge and walking fast again. It's not fair. You accepted all this just as I did, and now you suddenly spring a change of mind. But you have gone too far. You can't change your mind now. You can't go back now. He would telephone.

He would telephone and say something. What? The very idea of his own impersonal telephone voice and her hesitating one — what was there to say? What would it cost? Well, he had money now. Next week he would worry about that when it was gone. Now he must find a tram to take him to the station. He could not help remembering as he sat down how he had felt yesterday, how he had ridden in a tram when everything shone, when every person he saw looked gilded with his joy, when this had seemed to him the most beautiful city in the world; 'the city of flowers and linen,' he had begun a poem to celebrate it, to celebrate the day. He looked at people and they smiled. Joy one can share. But now their faces were shut against him. They looked satisfied or self-absorbed or bitter. Pain is personal. One suffers it alone. He could go up to a gendarme and say, 'Where is a florist?' but to say, 'I'm in despair. Where is a telephone?' That he could not do.

Everything obstructed his end. The tram was full and he had to squeeze himself onto the platform. When he got to the square a workman misdirected him and he had to walk back round another way to a side entrance of the station, into a dank room with no windows, a row of booths, and two wickets with 'Telephone — Telefoon' written up on them. He did not think what he would say. He thought only of saying it. He thought only of the telephone number and the mechanics of getting through to London, wondering if he would have to wait very long and for a second balancing on the abyss: she might be out. Manuele might be there. Lunch time.

'I want to telephone London.'

'Yes, Monsieur.' There seemed to be only one telephone in the office which the man left unhooked now and then and forgot about. Mark gave him the number with a feeling of despair. In this man's hands is the power to bring Georgia to me. He should look like a messenger of the gods: the man had a tobacco-stained moustache, a dirty celluloid collar, and a stringy black tie. He looked at Mark without interest and repeated the number in a nasal voice.

'You will have to wait.' Mark went over to the corner and sat on a stool. From here he could at least see the telephone. Every time it rang he got up as if he had been shot. Finally the man grunted:

'You needn't be so impatient, Monsieur. It takes at least twenty minutes.'

Mark sat down again. He felt sick. His eyes were fastened to the telephone as if connected by two wires. He did not think. He waited. He was simply a unit of waiting: a cat on its stomach waiting for the mouse to come out of the hole. Every now and then he turned his head to watch the minutes crawl across the face of the great clock — a useless gesture, because after an eternity there was a click each time and that was the hand moving. His emotions were single, focussed on the man with the moustache. When he went away from the telephone, leaving it carelessly and paying no attention to the imperative buzz, Mark was so angry that it became unbearable. When the man sauntered over and picked up the receiver his anger vanished before the suspense. This process went on and on until it seemed to Mark that he had been there a day and a night and he did not care any more whether Georgia was in or out; he simply wanted to be finished with it, to be free of it. When it finally happened, it happened so quickly that Mark had just time to precipitate himself into booth four.

'Hello, hello?' very faint on the other end of the wire came a voice.

'Who do you want to speak to?'

'Mrs. Conti, please,' he shouted into the telephone, but had the feeling that he was not reaching the ear at the other end.

'This is Mrs. Conti.'

'This is Mark,' he shouted, and then, without stopping to think what he was saying: 'I've got to see you.'

'W-w-w-wait a minute. I'm going upstairs. Hang on.' She disappeared. No one. Where was she? She couldn't take so long to go upstairs.

'Hello? Here I am. What did you say?' The long-distance telephone voice.

'Darling, I've got to see you. Your letter was a nightmare.'

'I'm sorry. I ——' She sounded so far away. There was no hope of reaching her.

'You've got to come here. Come for a day, just one day,' he said very loudly and clearly. The thing was to be heard. It would be enough.

'I can't, my darling. It's impossible.'

'You must. You must.' (Was he screaming into the telephone? The booth reeled around him. In the whole world there was nothing but this black object in his hand, this black tube to cling to with the other.) 'M for mother, U for Ukraine, S for Soap, T for Thomas — *Must!* (Was he laughing hysterically or crying?)

'All right. I will. The week-end. Good-bye.' She had hung up. She had sounded furious, exasperated. He had extorted this from her. It was done. But Mark did not feel elated. He felt lonely. This is hopeless. She is coming and it is hopeless. But already he was thinking: We will walk along the quais. We will go and look at the Van Eyck together.

'How much is it?

'Forty-five francs, Monsieur.' Mark took out his wallet. That left two hundred, a little over. Until the week-end he would go easy. It was done. There was nothing to be decided. After the week-end he could starve or steal, it didn't matter.

Georgia sat on her bed. Why had she said she would go? Something in his voice as if it were going to break, something in her that had felt 'I don't want to have to explain any more in letters,' and then the horror of the telephone, anything not to have to go on talking to someone she couldn't see across such a great distance. She sat on her bed, pulling threads out of the counterpane. She felt deeply irritated; she would have liked to tear the counterpane up into little pieces with irritation. She was caught. She did not want to be loved this morning. She did not want to be pleaded with or touched. She had begun a landscape. It was the shore, a place she had seen in Cornwall as a child, fields of wheat rolling down to a cliff and then the sea very green, very far below. At the foot of the cliff, a village, gray huddled houses and a great sea wall. There would be two figures alone in the landscape. They would be very small and yet the space between them would draw the eye, an allegory of partings and meetings. Two figures in a huge triumphant landscape, two figures speaking of desolation and joy, speaking of the spaces between people.

And now she was thrust back from this clear vision to the fragmentary, imperfect personal world. A mass of details confronted her. She must find some way of explaining to Manuele. She must see about tickets, about times. Above all she must be very clear in herself. She must know what she was doing. She must know her heart well. In some curious way she found herself responsible for a human heart, she found herself forced to answer 'Yes' when a boy's voice miles away said 'You must come.' She resented being responsible. It is peace that I want, and to finish this landscape. But she had not forgotten the black hair or the shape of the ear or the weight of his thin taut body against hers, and it was that, sending lightning up through her arteries, that forced her to her feet and down the stairs.

Manuele was eating his dessert. He looked so composed, so quiet as he looked up.

'Well?' For just a second as she sat down and folded her napkin neatly onto her knee, she hung in space thinking, What am I going to say?

'Oh, it was some crazy woman in Brussels' (did he know that Mark was in Ghent?) 'who wants me to do a portrait, a friend of the Hampshires.'

'Extraordinary to call you up long-distance. Why the hurry?'

'She wants it for a birthday present for her husband. I'll have to go there on the week-end. She'll have to be satisfied with a sketch.' (How easy it is to lie once one has begun.)

'Most extraordinary,' said Manuele. 'You should have let me talk to her. I'd have ticked her off. What does she think you are? A paper-hanger that she can call you long distance and say 'I want a portrait this morning, tomorrow'? Manuele was smiling at her across the table, across the white cups and saucers. A streak of sun lay just between them, a brilliant bar of sunlight and dazzling white china.

'The sun looks like a sword between us,' she murmured. Everything in the melodrama of this morning had become edged with meaning. She felt she could not look up over the streak of sun. She could not find his eyes. She felt so transparently a liar that she could not believe this was real, that he was really angry with this imaginary woman.

'I'll come with you,' he announced crossly, 'and I shall make the terms.'

'No, darling. Don't be silly.' (Oh, God, get me out of this. A Catholic, she thought, would have the satisfaction of promising a candle, but she must manage without heavenly protection.) 'I'll only be away three nights, and I should be too agitated if you were growling around. Besides, I need the money — it's really quite a godsend.'

'Well —— ' His tone assumed that he was not coming. 'Make her pay for her cheek.'

'I will. Don't worry.' In the relief, the gratitude that swept over her, the band of sunlight between them became unbearable. She got up and went over to him: 'Oh, Manuele, what a complicated business life is!' (I wish I could tell you the truth.) 'Now I must bother about tickets and all that and call up the Beatons and put off the week-end, and I was so well started on the landscape.'

'I'll do all that, you silly woman.'

'I hate leaving you,' she said, 'but I must fly. I'm going to work like a demon all morning. Good-bye, my darling.'

'Work well,' he said, picking up the paper.

Work well. It was like a blessing. Work well, it sang in her mind. It was done. As easily as that. This is how people deceive their husbands. This is how simple it is to lie. And suddenly she felt that if this were possible and she could go to Belgium to see Mark with no one knowing, then she must be surrounded with such lies. One can believe nothing, she thought. Everything must be deception. It seemed no longer possible to go back to the simple purity of her allegory. It was as if a film lay between her and the simple truth, the truth.

Was it better, she wondered, to take the lie on oneself, to dull the integral vision to spare someone else? For what in the end is the truth? Was it perhaps not only sparing Manuele but in the end true, what she was doing; for it is Manuele whom I love, she thought, taking a dress out of the cupboard and thinking, This is what I shall wear. Even as she stopped a moment to rearrange the roses, that is the truth, she decided, and what I have done to Mark and myself is the lie. And it is that I must tell Mark, she thought, bending to smell the roses and then putting them aside, setting them on the mantelpiece as if there were something to be denied in this sweetness that opened the veins and made her feel again that summer dizziness, that curious fatigue of the past two weeks.

Chapter Five

THE blackbird was singing in anticipation of the cherries, which were still hard green stones but which he had already pecked here and there to see how they were getting along. Pascal lay under the hedge thinking; this was visible in the luminous stare of his eyes and in the slow uncurling and curling of his tail. It was a very active stillness. Over the strawberry bed and among the roses and pinks there was a continual murmur of bees and occasionally the brilliant zigzag flight of a dragon fly. The white table and the three chairs sat like gentle reminders that even with all this life in it the garden lacked something, and all this was only the frame for three figures sitting with the sun falling in abrupt light and shadow on their faces, or stooping among the strawberries and occasionally going off into gales of laughter, and then as suddenly sighing.

Mark had found his way into the alley at the back and was stretching his neck to see over the high stone walls and heavy barred gates to find the garden. From a distance he saw a hawthorn bush and a wire gate that let you look in. No, there couldn't be two gardens with such a bed of strawberries, with such a wall of gooseberries. But did he dare push open the gate and go in this secret way? It was so still in the sun he thought his feet would sound marauding. The gate pushed open silently. There, he was in. And the minute he was in, the spell of this particular world fell on him. The day and the night had passed so slowly until now. He had felt numb and tired, unable to work, unable even to think. There had been a blight on the day. Because Georgia was coming he could think of nothing else, and because he had forced her to come he could not think of her without a feeling of blight. But as he closed the gate behind him and stooped to pick a handful of strawberries, it was as if a spell worked, a charm enveloped him. The sun on his neck crept down his spine like a warm liquor. He picked the strawberries slowly, lifting the leaves one by one, and peering underneath to the nests of vermilion. When his cupped hand was full he got up.

He got up and walked up the path under the cherry tree to the door of the dining-room. The house looked very still. He looked up at Doro's window, but there was no one there. In the other room Doro had laid out a pile of little objects: from the bottoms of drawers and the top shelves of cupboards she had been hunting treasures, and now they lay on her table, two Japanese prints, three small yellow-backed books signed Jean Latour, a lacquer pencil Pierre had brought her back from Japan. Just behind them on the desk stood a jar with the lilies of the valley and forget-me-nots standing in it. Together these objects spoke of so much joy that it seemed as if nothing else were necessary, but every few seconds she stepped swiftly over to the window and pulled back the curtain to see if anyone was coming.

Mark hesitated at the big door to the dining-room and then turned to the side where he could hear someone singing. Marthe was ironing. She jumped when she saw a handsome boy go past her window — the boy of the day before, Mamzelle Doro's boy. She ran to open the door.

'Oh, Monsieur,' she said (it was an ovation). 'You are looking for the way in. Come through the kitchen.'

'Thank you so much. May I come in this way? I have been stealing strawberries.'

'Oh, Monsieur,' said Marthe again, overcome with embarrassment and pleasure. 'I'll just tell Mamzelle you're here. She's expecting you.' He thought of his hotel room where he had sat half the morning with his head in his hands on the unmade bed, and blessed this house where he was expected.

'I'll find my way up.' He ran up the stairs two at a time and knocked at the study door. No answer. Then he heard a rustle behind him. Doro had opened her bedroom door and stood just behind him.

'Hello! Have a strawberry, one of your own strawberries?'

'Oh!' She bent down and took one out of his hand. He thought, She is so like a bird.

'How are you?' said Mark. 'Did you sleep well?'

'Have you brought me the poem? Come along; come in or we shall stand talking in the hall forever.'

'There is so much to say and I just want to be silent. I just want to look at you.'

'Come and sit down.' This time he sat in the little chair and Doro in the armchair. For just a second he met her eyes. In that second he felt he had been a long journey. For a moment there was nothing to say.

'Here is the poem,' he said then, but his voice sounded to him like a strange voice. The tone had altered. Something had entered into his voice, another voice, and changed it.

'But we can't read it now,' she said, 'for we have forgotten about lunch.' But we'll have the whole afternoon. You will rest here on my bed after lunch and then you will read to me.' She thought he must rest. Why does he look so tired?

'And you, you must rest a little too,' he said in a dreamy voice. He felt as if he were asleep and resting.

'Yes, yes,' she said, knowing that she could never rest with this wild creature in her room and that she would not want to rest. 'Have you been working this morning?'

'No, I sat on my bed and wished I were dead.' He laughed at the unintentional rhyme which made the morning seem ridiculous now.

'It's strange. All the time I was reading to the children this morning, I felt so troubled. I felt as if I were walking beside you invisible and that something terrible was happening to you. Perhaps I bungled the lesson among the Greeks, but never mind. They know the stress of these tempests the soul suffers like a sea — they'll forgive me,' she said, smiling at him. 'And now tell me, what is it?' She watched his curious impatient gesture, his hand rubbing his forehead as if he were rubbing something away, smoothing out a knot behind it.

'Something I didn't tell you yesterday.'

'I know. What is it? I want to know everything,' she said simply.

'I want to tell you,' he began. 'It's because I'm in love,' he said.

'I know.' She felt that in the last few minutes she had become in an extraordinary way a projection of him, or that he was a projection of her. She felt as if she could guess everything he was going to say before he said it.

'She is married. She is in love with her husband,' Mark felt it only necessary to say four or five words. She would know the rest. She would see it through him, through herself.

This was a terrible thing he was telling her. Doro saw how young he was, how he was still made all of intensity and impatience, how he would burn like a bonfire suddenly and not know what he was doing, what just now he had said and the implications of it. But he was going on quietly: 'It happened so suddenly that there was no time to think, so perfectly that I built a whole world on it, so apparently inevitably that it seemed as if it were something I had been expecting all my life.'

'Yes, yes,' said Doro softly, 'I know.' How difficult it is to distinguish in the middle of these bonfires which are temporary; how many one must suffer before one can measure, before one knows. She thought: He will have to go through all that. Even I cannot give him experience in a parcel, cannot save him from every inch of the way that he must go.

'Now she is coming here for the week-end. But something has happened. She wrote me such a strange letter — it's in her that something has happened. She has begun to think.' He spoke in short quick sentences, as if this were an algebraic equation and from the single numbers she would discover the *x*.

'Who is she?' said Doro, thinking she must have an image on which to fasten her thoughts, thinking to be wise one must first know a great deal, and although everything is the same nothing is quite the same.

'She is a painter. Years ago I saw a landscape of hers. I wanted to buy it.' So, thought Doro thinking of another painter, everything has a pattern. These are the miracles. This is the way things happen again and again, the way the heart is fashioned.

'She is tall. She has a still, carved face. She moves like a swan: she is like a swan, awkward and graceful all at once. She has fine red hair, like a Memling madonna.'

'Yes, yes,' she said, 'I see her very well,' saying nothing more for now she must listen. She must let him pour it all out little by little.

As Mark talked it was again as if he saw everything in perspective. By the way Doro listened she made everything seem simple. By the way she listened he saw that she took it for granted that these things were living, that one must love, that one must walk with an abyss on every side, that one must suffer. Nothing astonished her. There was nothing he could say, he felt, that she had not known and weighed already to its greatest possible depth. And as he talked he saw that everything was good, that everything that would happen to him now and for years to come would be like this, difficult and painful and in the end necessary. But she was speaking now.

'Everything is possible except the suffering of others,

except the ruthlessness of passion that spreads like a poison, touching the innocent always'; and he thought of Manuele and his lean, watchful face, and he was glad that Georgia had written as she did, blessed her for knowing what she did, for keeping him from a fearful thing. Though he must hold her in his arms once more, he thought; he must have her still for a little while.

'How good it is to be here,' he said. 'How simple everything becomes in this room' — though he knew that only for a moment would he be able to enter this garden, that only at moments would it seem good to love Georgia and ask for nothing, that only now because he was sitting in the little red chair would life seem grand enough to make everything seem possible, everything worth a great price.

They sat silent for a moment, Doro looking out over his head, and then she said: 'Come, you must look at my treasures. I have found some treasures for you.'

'Oh!' She was standing at the table holding out to him a thin blue paper, a Japanese paper. He took it and saw Hiroshige's night, a bridge over a river full of little boats setting off fireworks, one single stream of light falling high over the rest and filling the sky with stars. 'Yes, it is beautiful,' he said. They both knew what it meant, how well it fitted the hour.

'There's the bell. We must go. You must be hungry.' Always they hesitated before making the transition between Doro's room and the great world of downstairs. This house, thought Mark, is like a series of Japanese boxes, one inside the other, each holding its secret.

'Well, here he is,' said Annette as he came over to shake her hand.

'I'm glad to see you,' he said; for it was true he had felt a rush of gladness at seeing them both and the table with its blue and white china; especially he was glad to see Clairette's blue eyes smiling at him. It was almost a relief to escape for a little while the curious nakedness of spirit he suffered with Doro. It was amusing to be back in a world where he could be at ease, where each word did not have to be weighed for its grain of truth.

'Well,' said Claire, looking around in triumph, 'you will never believe it, but André has learned the present participle and the past participle at last.'

'I believe it,' said Annette. 'Considering the extent and number of bribes he has received in the shape of the best bonbons to be found, he will be utterly spoiled.'

'Ah, but he will pass his examination,' said Doro with a twinkle.

'Mark has nothing to eat, poor boy,' said Annette, picking up his plate and heaping it with chicken and salad. 'It is a great day when we have chicken for lunch; you had better take advantage of it.'

Mark laughed. He looked happily at them each eating tiny mouthfuls, and he thought that they were like little owls, exactly.

With the chicken they laughed, they teased each other, and Mark felt that he was really at home for the first time in his life, and this consisted in being able to eat his chicken bone with his fingers; it consisted in having Clairette opposite him and Annette to chase out of her chair and round the table; it consisted in not daring too often to look over at Doro, but in the occasional swift glance which said: 'You are there. It is true.'

With the chicken they laughed; with the strawberries

a silence fell upon them which was partly a silence of strawberries and partly the silence before a cigarette, before a conversation. And with the coffee Clairette asked him questions about his poem and he sat and talked, sat and explained it to them happily. They talked of writing in general and the problems of a writer in a small country, and as Mark listened to Clairette he felt the sort of awe that a very strong charm exerts.

'You will stay for tea — we shall see you then?' she said graciously as they got up to go upstairs. Doro smiled a curious smile of her own that he had seen once or twice, as if she were tasting her own smile and it was both bitter and sweet.

'Come, let us go,' he said, going over to her and taking her arm; for suddenly as she smiled he felt: I must go over and be sure she is there, that we are together. So, when one is not assured by a look, by a small gesture that love is present, that it has not vanished, one is always in suspense, one always wonders, 'Is it real?' They walked up the stairs with the slowing up of tempo which spells afternoon in contradistinction to morning.

'They are darlings,' he said as they stopped on the landing. She led the way to her room as if this were a march of triumph, this brief walk together up a flight of stairs.

As they found themselves back in the room it swept over him that he had come here and accepted everything too gladly and too easily. He had filled his arms with flowers, and laughed without thinking how deeply he was given, how deeply he was attaching himself here. And he saw in the moment it took her to walk to the window and pull the curtains that they would always be standing on the edge of an abyss, that she would die, soon, long before him. And he felt the huge gulf of time between them for the first time in thinking of her death.

'I know,' she said, standing by the window as if she had read his thoughts. 'But you mustn't think of that. Come, you are going to sleep a little while on the sofa.' It was true that he was tired, so tired that his eyes half closed as she spoke. Once more he remembered the sensation he had of coming to the end of a long journey, that he was coming, as he met her glance, from very far away, very near. It was tiring.

'And you?' he said as she put a quilt over him and he shut his eyes.

'I shall go into the other room if I want to.' He was slipping down into sleep, feeling as if he were lying out under a great sky full of stars.

Chapter Six

GEORGIA'S train was due at half-past seven. At half-past seven it was still just five minutes out. She felt dazed and disheveled and dirty. It had been a rough trip across the Channel; she had tried to sleep but couldn't. The journey had been an unpleasant limbo in which she could no longer escape into ordering the dinner, into arranging the flowers. She had had six hours in which the same thoughts wove themselves back and forth through her mind without stopping like shuttles. Now as she powdered her nose and made the careful vermilion line of her mouth she felt incapable of facing any situation. If I only felt as I looked, she thought. For what the man opposite her saw was an attractive woman putting on her gloves, a nice middle-class Englishwoman going to stay with an aunt in Ghent or perhaps sketch. Inside she wished she could just lie down somewhere in a wood with Mark and sleep. But it was no good thinking of that. He would be there standing on the platform with his strained face, waiting for a word, waiting for her to say, 'I do not love you.'

She began to be really nervous with an ache in the pit of her stomach. She had smoked so much that her mouth felt woolly, but she took out a cigarette. The man opposite produced a lighter. It was startling as the train slowed down to be confronted with a strange man holding out a light. I suppose he has been here all this time, she thought, and wondered what had been written on her face.

'Thank you.'

At half-past seven Mark was standing on the platform with his hands in his pockets. The train would be five minutes late. Now that the moment had at last arrived (all day he had expected a telegram saying she couldn't come), he felt perfectly calm as if in fact everything had happened already and he were simply present at a rehearsal of the past. It was alarming not to remember her face more exactly. It would be terrible if he didn't recognize her. He was walking up and down saying to himself: 'Now it will come. In one minute this will be over. You will never have to live through it again'; and even before the minute had ticked itself away on the face of the big clock the red lights of the engine swerved in, rushed into the station panting as if it could never stop. Always his heart jumped right up into his mouth at the sight of a train coming into a station. There was a moment of confusion. Just my luck, he thought, that there seems to be an army getting out; he supposed Georgia would be travelling second, but he couldn't see a single second-class carriage. Already swarms of soldiers were pouring down the stairs. Suppose he had missed her. He hesitated whether to run down and make sure, but then he would surely miss her.

Georgia waited for a porter (the man had gone to get her one). Leaning out of the window she thought, 'I shall never find him in this mob.' One couldn't separate one person from another. She leaned far out and looked up and down.

'Hello!' He was standing behind her in the carriage.

'Oh, what are you doing here?'

'I saw you leaning out of the window, had just about decided that you weren't on the train. Come along or we'll get caught.'

'I thought we'd surely miss each other. It's good to see you,' she said quickly and under her breath, as she always did when she was nervous. They had not even shaken hands. They had not yet begun to play their parts. They felt there was something horribly wrong, a wall of strangeness, a situation between them.

'I'll get you a porter,' he said, and rushed away, though she had only one bag.

She is looking awful. But I love her. I love her, he thought as he shouted, 'Hey, porteur, par ici!'

Georgia was sitting on a bench when he came back.

'I feel quite dazed,' she said as they went down the stairs.

'You must be starving. I hope you won't mind staying at my dingy hotel. I reserved a room for you.' Georgia blinked as they came out onto the square.

'I haven't been here for years,' she murmured, but she felt incapable of coping with a city. People seemed to be bustling about so, to know exactly where they were going. Only I don't know where I'm going, she thought, stepping off the pavement onto the street and just avoiding a beer-wagon.

'Darling, look out!' They were crossing the square. (It's true, Mark said something to me just now and I didn't hear it.)

'Oh, yes, I shall love to stay at your hotel — is this our street?' She was grateful for the narrowness, the darkness. She looked at Mark for the first time. Looking at him walking beside her with his restless eager expression, for he was talking steadily now, she thought how fond she was of him.

'We're almost there. It's an awful hole really, but the people are nice.' He was talking steadily because as they got nearer his agitation mounted. The nice patronne was here smiling and greeting them. It was a comfort to be welcomed so warmly. She took the bags and put them in the elevator.

'Let's walk up,' he said to Georgia. 'It's just one flight.'

'Oh, Monsieur, aren't you going to take the elevator?' said the concierge. (It was the elevator, no doubt, that made the hotel 'même chic').

'No, thank you.'

'Ah, Monsieur prefers to walk,' she said with an understanding expression, as if there were some obscure amorous English reason for walking upstairs with a lady.

'I hope it will be all right,' he said anxiously to Georgia.

'Of course it will.' They were shown into a smallish brown room which seemed to contain nothing but the double bed hidden under a huge rose puff. 'It is splendid. I shall feel like a Wagnerian heroine — who is it in Parsifal who is hoisted across the stage on a bed of roses?' She was opening a little case and taking out bottles. 'Where are you?'

'Right up at the top. Because I can see the sky,' he

added as if there could be no other reason, as if he could afford this sumptuous room if he wanted it.

'I must come and see you. Tell me the number and I'll come up in a few minutes. I want to see where you live — and I must do something to my face. I can't bear that you should see me looking like such a hag, see?' She took his hand.

'You're beautiful and I adore you,' he said, but she had turned back to the case, to the bottles. On purpose? He would not believe it. Such a stream of happiness flooded him as he watched her bend, the line of her neck, her strong hands that he had forgotten.

He is standing there, she thought, and though I have managed once to turn away, to resist, it is going to be so difficult to go on.

'Come soon,' he said, and shut the door, running up the stairs full of this secret joy, not believing yet, not wanting to believe that she could have come for any other reason but this one. And it is charming, he thought, that she must first powder her nose before she kisses me.

Georgia was so glad to be alone for one moment that she sat down on the bed and sighed with relief. I'm a fool to have come, she thought. How can one expect him to understand? I cross the channel. I lie to my husband and stay at Mark's hotel for the night. How can he understand that I have come here to tell him something instead of writing it? She got up and went to the basin to pour cold water over her face, to wash her hands. One might as well have clean hands to commit the murder. It seemed all wrong to have to tell him such a thing. Why not wait until tomorrow, tell him tomorrow? She met her eyes in the mirror. She met herself and stared incredulously at a woman in a hotel room, an unscrupulous woman who was about to deceive not only her husband but herself and Mark, Mark with his unnatural intensity. It was a relief to get away from the mirror and not to have to face herself any longer. I must go and tell him now.

'So this is where you live,' Georgia said, sitting on the bed and swinging her legs. But it is such a dreary room, she thought. I must get him some flowers. She noticed his shaving brush and soap and the comb on the glass shelf above the basin. For some reason they looked in themselves infinitely lonely. I should weep in this room, she thought — the brown walls, the tiny window. And then she caught his eyes watching her. He must not think for a moment that I am sorry for him.

'My darling, you should have been a monk — such austerity!'

'Should I? That's a dangerous thing to say, you incredible woman! Are you here? Is this my room?' He said, standing where he was against the wall and thinking he would not kiss her yet, maintain this delicious suspense a little longer, this torture, this delight: 'Is it really you?'

'It's I, and I'm starving. Let's go and eat.'

'It's so good to see you. Let me look at you.' For now suddenly, and his voice told it plainly, it seemed stupid to play the game any longer when this wonder was here for them to taste. He came over and put his hand on her shoulder. There they were, the same clear eyes, the pupils opening, like looking down into ice.

(He is going to kiss me and I mustn't let him.) 'Come along, darling,' she said quickly, 'let's go.'

'But Georgia, Georgia, you haven't kissed me — you have very clumsily turned away and spoiled that kiss.'

'I can't.'

There, it was said. She sat with her hands in her lap waiting. The room flew apart. The walls vanished. We are sitting in a vast silence. I can't look at him. I can't move.

Mark stood looking down at the strong hands, suddenly pitiful in her lap, as if she had abandoned them. In one second something has happened. Something has happened, but I can only stand here and look down at her head bent and the shape of her hands. It was as if the words she had said were taking a long time to reach his ear, were travelling like star light, millions of miles, and then they reached him. She said, 'I can't.' He heard it.

'But Georgia, why? You haven't come all this way to tell me that? You can't. You can't do such things. What do you think I am, a block of wood, that you can come all this way and sit on my bed and say such things?' Now he was only angry. Why did she sit there so patiently, so pitifully? He hated women in that moment with their terrible power of calling out pity, of being meek, of committing the murder and then weeping, for as he watched he saw a tear roll down her cheek, and she did not move.

Now he hates me and he is right. She did not move; she could see nothing but his hand relaxed, contradicting the anger in his voice, speaking of despair, and she thought: If I could only take it, but I can't. Because there is his pride. And I cannot comfort him now. I must not touch him ever again with a soft word. The tears came one by one and rolled down her cheeks.

'You cry so well,' he said bitterly. 'Here is my handkerchief.'

But I must speak to him, she thought. I must because I love him now better than ever before. And he must know. He must understand.

'Mark,' she said. 'Mark.' Then he was kneeling on the floor beside her with his head against her knees saying in a funny thin voice:

'Yes, tell me. I want to know.'

'It's just that one can't love two people in the same way, my darling.' (Yes, yes, I see, and I see too because of this and because I respect you more now for feeling it and understand you better, that you have disarmed me. There is no weapon that can be used against integrity, none that I would use.)

'I had to find out, you see. I didn't know.'

'Until I had left. Yes, I understand.' (Ah, God, this tyranny of the flesh, this weakness of the spirit!) 'But why didn't you tell me in your letter, why did you use half words — why, why did you come?' He asked, for it was horrible to be exposed here to this pity. One should be alone; one should be allowed to go and hide like an animal, he thought.

'Because I'm a fool,' she said simply, 'and because I love you, love you more now, if you only knew, than I ever have before' (because now I am free, I am no longer taking part in a battle with you and with myself).

'Here is my handkerchief,' he said gently. 'You had better blow your nose. And then we must have some food.' He got up. 'I do understand. I understand,' he said again, as if he could go no further. 'Thank you for coming.'

'My dear.' She stood and put her arms round him. She held him close to her and did not let him go, though he struggled. And he struggled because across miles of conflict and war and suspense here at last was the end of the journey. Here was communion. Now in this grief and in this parting they had arrived. He struggled because he was ashamed to let her see his tears.

'Cry. Do cry.'

'It's only because,' he said, brushing the tears away, 'because I'm so happy.' (But I cannot explain why I'm so happy or what it is, when everything has been taken away, that I possess it all. Is it because, he thought, love has no appointed hour or season. Is it when grief abounds without desire, when the heart burns like a desert without flowers, that it is suddenly revealed?)

And Georgia thought: He is more beautiful and better than I had dreamed. They went out like lovers, to find somewhere in the strange city to eat.

There was everything to talk about. They sat in a café drinking coarse red wine, eating an omelette and a salad, relishing it, agreeing that it was these simple things that made life worth living. Mark watched her. Everything had now become an end in itself and not a terrible state of suspension. They were here together. It was enough. Because one door was shut another door had opened: they were in an entirely different world, making the world of passion seem small, passion that consumes everything else, that sets everything up only in relation to itself.

They had never laughed together before. Now everything amused them: the assiduity of the waiter to light Georgia's cigarettes, the cocotte behind them with her young man, who was undoubtedly, they decided, a bicycle racer, the orchestra playing Tchaikovsky's 'Valse Triste.' Even that made them laugh because it was so badly played.

'You know,' she said, 'I've never known you before. I've never,' she said, laughing, 'really looked at you before.'

'No, we were someone else — a third person.'

'I'm so happy and so grateful,' she said, looking at him over her wineglass, setting it down to look at him. I'm so grateful to be alive, she thought, to be drinking sour red wine in a café.

'Go on with your story. What happened then?' he asked, because she had begun to tell him about Manuele. She told him that they had met in Florence when she was just beginning to paint. He was a dealer from Rome. She had asked him to look at her sketches and he had refused because he was so sure that they would be bad. And then one day he found her painting in a field and he said, 'But you can paint.' She would never forget the surprise in his voice.

Mark listened, listened as if he were transparent and the words could pass into him like wine, like bread. This was a gift she was making him. She was giving him herself at last.

They talked of writing and painting, of the curious necessity to produce one's inner world, to bring it out and exhibit it.

'Are you ever terrified that you won't be able to paint again?'

'Every day.'

'So am I. It's so strange. I suppose it's one's terror that the vision will fail. I'm never afraid that I won't be able to write. I'm only afraid that suddenly there will be no reason for writing any more. As if one were the man who saw the burning bush and must tell. If there were no fire in one's path one would simply go home to bed.'

'I wonder. With me it's that I can never tell the vision — it's the means which I lack,' she said, looking down.

'M-m-m. That's because you're an artist and I'm not,' he said happily. 'Let's have some coffee.'

They had talked and now they were silent. It was good to sit opposite each other and drink their coffee, sip it, listen to the band playing four-year-old jazz as if it were Mendelssohn — 'Smoke Gets in Your Eyes.'

'Ouf! That reminds me of Nice,' said Mark. 'Let's go.'

'This is Dutch,' said Georgia definitely.

'Don't be silly.' Mark took out his last hundred francs.

That is the only bill in his wallet, thought Georgia. But in spite of that, because of it, perhaps, I must let him pay the bill though I am rich and he is poor. She felt sad thinking what a cruel inviolable thing is pride.

They went out separately through the swinging door. It was raining. The lights looked blurred in the rain and melted into themselves.

'You'll get wet,' he said, taking her arm.

'It doesn't matter. Rain is our element, I think.'

'Yes. Let's walk.' They walked without speaking

along the dark street splotched with light. The warmth of the café was gone. They were alone in the street. And they dreaded going back to the hotel, as if they were carrying such a fragile thing in their hands the least shock might smash it. Georgia decided, I must say something now or when we are there I shall be too overpowered by the brown wallpaper.

'I dread going back to the hotel,' he said aloud.

'I know, I know. Oh, Mark, don't go away by yourself. Come and stay with me tonight, just quietly, just to rest even if you can't sleep.' Once it was said, she thought, Perhaps I am sticking a spear down into him. Perhaps I am asking too much, and because I do not want him to go away I am asking him an extraordinary, an impossible thing. 'I suppose one doesn't ask that sort of thing,' she added, dropping his arm. 'Forgive me.'

They walked along in silence. But Mark was silent because he could not speak, because a kind of sickness of relief was on him.

'No, no, you're dear. You understand everything,' he said finally. The words fell into the rain, into the silence, like rain, like mercy, she thought.

This is the first time that I'm young, really young, and she is ten years older since we've met. It's strange. It's all right.

'Bonsoir.' The concierge's warm smile enveloped them.

He left her at her door. 'I'll come down in a little while. How happy the concierge will be when she finds my bed made up tomorrow morning,' he laughed. She could hear him laughing to himself on the flight above, running like a boy to the flight above.

When he knocked on the door Georgia was sitting up in bed with her long fine hair falling straight down her shoulders.

'Oh, Georgia, you look like Mélisande, you look so sweet,' he said, burying his face in her hair.

'My darling.' It didn't matter a bit that he wouldn't sleep, he did not want to sleep — and he thought there will be time enough, all the rest of my life to sleep in. Now he wanted to lie holding her hand with his eyes shut, remembering how he had pushed open door after door, how he had sat in her house, hunting for her vainly. It was sweet to lie awake for a night, now that he had found her at last.

Chapter Seven

DORO sat on the sofa in the room looking out into the garden. The cherry tree was so thick now that she could just see the edge of the white table; the bench was quite hidden, and only a sewing basket and a red spool betrayed that under the leaves someone was sitting — Clairette, for Annie had taken the children on an excursion. These days went by so fast that Doro could not count them. It seemed as if there were never enough time in which to do nothing, in which to *be*. One must have time to prepare oneself, and then one must have time afterwards to taste experience, to explore it, to remember. This morning she had read the older children Claudel's 'L'Otage.' She had read it well. She had taken the words and clothed herself in them as in a magnificent dress; she had been intoxicated with the sense of power in her own voice. And then she had come up here where she could sit and look out, where she could sort out the multitude of sensations, of ideas, of emotions that Mark had exploded in her by walking into the room looking so like the Watteau Gilles and saying, 'You are Jean Latour.'

She thought how curious it is that one can never share these experiences. She could give him her love. He could give her his. They could share laughter, a game, tenderness, a moment when they were both moved by a quality of light, by a shadow, but at the centre and the nearer they came to the heart, the wider the abyss between them.

She sat looking down through the thick leaves where she could just see Clairette's toe now in a white shoe (the red spool on the table had vanished), and she thought, When the thing happens, when suddenly the poem is life, when the Gilles walks into the room and sits down beside you, there is nothing to say and one has no desire to speak. There is such sweetness in not talking about those one loves, of withdrawing round them into a deep wordless thought so that nothing will be lost — so that silence may accompany the experience like an intense inner music.

She sat looking down, and Clairette's toe tapped impatiently. I must go down, she thought. I must go down and see how Clairette is. For if it is true that we do not want to speak of it, still we want to pour out the sweetness — we must go and share what we have in our hands.

She pushed open the big door into the garden, sliding the bolt back. She did it so quietly that Clairette only looked up when she was standing beside her.

'Hello, my dear,' said Doro. 'I am coming to sit here if I may.'

The sun fell in splotches on the table. From where she sat Doro could smell the pinks.

'What have you been doing?' asked Claire, while the needle went in and out of the stocking she was mending.

'Sitting at my window looking down at you, at your white foot, which was all I could see of you. I wanted to come down and sit beside you for a little while'; for everything that filled her hands, she saw now, could not be talked about, could not be shared, however much she wanted to.

Clairette sighed and put down her needle. She turned to Doro and looked at her sitting there with her head in her hands, and she thought, 'What a child she is!'

'Oh, Clairette,' said Doro, as if her voice were only the continuation of the sound of summer in the leaves, as if, Clairette thought, as she listened, her voice were part of the bees and the smell of pinks coming softly out of the air, 'for the first time in my life I am not afraid of death, isn't it strange? I am not afraid of dying.'

'No,' said Clairette, turning her blue eyes on her for the first time. 'No, I think I understand.'

'Bless you,' said Doro, and kissed Clairette's hand. She could only make a humble gesture. She could only kiss Clairette's hand as those who are happy must kiss the hands of those who are not.

There had been a little wind. Now no leaf stirred. The air smelled of warm grass and pinks. Somewhere someone was raking. The sound served to point the silence of this garden.

So it is that the miracles of the spirit take place, always unexpected, never in the moment of anguish, of despair, but quite simply when one has ceased to demand the miracle, when one accepts.

Doro did not want to move. She wanted to be quite still. She knew that even the vision which comes quietly and after long waiting must strain the heart. She felt incandescent, and she knew too well what that meant. She wondered how long the waves of dizziness would hold off, and whether life would be so gracious as to give her this afternoon with Mark — for there was something that she must tell him still.

Chapter Eight

THIS afternoon there was no question of a shadow at the window. Doro leaned far out and waved as Mark came into sight. She had been sitting saying over his poem as if from the sound she could extract the meaning, and it seemed to her as if she had, as if now she held it in her hands, and it had been born by some prodigy of intuition, complete in her mind. She wanted to talk to him about it quickly before this state of inner brilliance broke into chaos.

Mark had slept for hours that seemed like days after Georgia left. When he woke up he felt fresh, as if a strain had been lifted. For the first time he was going to see Doro, a free man, bringing Georgia with him, not having to bury her carefully under layers of other things, not having to hide the subterranean pull that had dragged him back each time at the instant of meeting, had made him say 'But Georgia ——,' had made him unable to think of the problem that had brought him here while this other, this personal struggle, was going on. He waved a bunch of roses in his hand and shouted, 'Hello!'

The door was open. He ran up the stairs three at a time.

Once in the room he threw the roses on the bed so that he could take both her hands in his and say 'Hello' again.

'Hello!' she said, laughing at the sound of this English exclamation.

Always it took some minutes for the excitement of meeting, the drums and trumpets of meeting, to die down. And then there was a pause. They sat, she in the low armchair, he on the little red chair. They sat and looked at each other while one by one the doors into the myriad rooms of the heart and mind closed softly and clicked and only the great door of silence opened to let them out. Then Doro said:

'I have been reading your poem.'

'Do you understand it?'

'I understand it all,' she said. 'You are a poet,' she said, looking away, thinking now I must speak. 'I love it for what it is and for its great promise,' she said, 'and I mean promise in the sense of something that you owe to us and to yourself here, a promise you are making in writing this poem. But,' she added, 'I think you're wrong. I think you're willing it into a shape and yourself into a shape that is not yours, and that is, because of that, false — why did you write it?'

'Because I felt ashamed of myself for living in this personal world, because it seemed to me that I must lose myself in something greater.' (This is what I have come for. This is why I have been drawn here. These are the words that had to be said to me sooner or later, he thought.) 'Because I was so sick of myself that I wanted to lose myself,' he said, holding his hands together as if he were extracting the truth out of the pressure of bone against bone.

'Yes,' she said, looking at the restless dark eyes that seemed to reach out and possess everything they looked upon. 'Read me a little — the first verses of the "Envoi," will you? And then I'll try to tell you what I think.'

As Mark picked up the sheets and shuffled them, looking for the beginning, which had got mixed up, he thought he had never wanted to do anything so much in his life. And he wondered if at the moment of reading his voice would not suddenly vanish. But he finally got the pages straightened out and began:

'Even last night the personal, the childish wonder
Hooded my eyes, blinded with its protection —
There was no earth, no horror but this dark silk under,
This dark silk over, holding the pale balloon and its reflection
Like a tired lover.'

Yes, he is a poet, she thought, but one sees it more in what is lacking in this poem. How full of effort it is, as if he were carrying a great weight over his imagination.

'Even last night the moon's attraction and its tyranny were all;
The elements still cherished and surrounded
Involuntary love and the despair was personal,
The world an ocean glittering with my love and bounded
By that emotion.'

He thought, she is sitting with one hand over her eyes and I can't see her face. I cannot tell whether she understands or is just listening to the shape of the poem. It is terrible to read a poem to someone who doesn't understand.

'Today I have risen from the self-inflicted tomb,
And in the Easter of the spirit shall accept the earth,
The horror and the inevitable growing pang in the womb,
The aching vision enlarged by this difficult birth
And the heart's division.'

But she thought, Everything in his face belies this. Everything in his face with its curious sternness speaks of a different struggle, a struggle to arrive at his personal truth, his personal solution. Everything in his face speaks of the mind and heart trying to speak together, not to lose themselves in a great camouflage of ideas. It is not this that he should be saying.

'Today I am parted from myself more deeply than by death.
I am terribly parted from the dark head and the kiss.
I have lost the multitude of loves and the wandering breath.
I am no longer one in a moonlike singleness
Reflecting the sun.'

It is curious, she thought, how well I understand this. I do not understand the words. I understand the meaning.

'For us the agony is this, the modern crucifixion
Happens in Spain or China and wherever the deluded man
Chooses his difference, his capital division:
The individual in hate or love is the hooded one,
Making war's ritual.'

How pompous this is, how naïve and pompous, he thought. One struggles to say something, and then one must listen to one's own voice afterwards repeating platitudes like a minister in a pulpit who no longer believes what he is saying.

'We must come to be many and no longer one alone,
We must come to a fresh perception of the heart's desire,
This is the meaning that will turn back the stone,
Turn us from the easy bed, the mind's conflict, and the bitter fire,
To rise from the dead.'

To rise from the dead, he thought, laying the bundles of paper down on the floor; to rise from the dead, the living dead.

Now I must speak, she thought; she was looking away out of the window. I must tell him why it is he had to come here just now, and what of me it is that he needs. For I see now that it is a definite thing.

He was aware that she was not looking at him. He felt the poem crumbling in his hands. But she did not say what he thought she was going to. She looked down at him as it seemed from a great distance, or as if from very far away, coming toward him as she looked as if she were crossing an ocean and at a certain moment would step onto his shore, a foreign shore.

'When you read your poems I feel a sort of anguish as if I could not suffice all this, support it — that I can only reach out at you from a great distance, the great distance of time between us. But I have never been able to believe,' she went on, 'that from a depersonalized, universalized being anything really human, any living form of art, could be born — because one can only give what one is, not what one thinks nor what one does nor what one would like to be: "Today I am parted from myself,"' she said hesitantly in English. 'That's just it. In this poem you are parted from yourself — you are trying to be something instead of being it. And death is the inevitable result for anyone who gives up his differences. Oh, Mark, don't doubt yourself. Don't think you can live in a great tent of longing or theory, or that because you ought to be something you must pretend to be it. Just lie down on a hill and look up at the stars.'

There, it was said. The words fell one by one like snowflakes between them. The silence that followed was like a snow silence, soft and absolute. Then Mark said,

'You know.'

'Yes, I have never for one moment doubted my heart, even if it has sometimes seemed to me a poor thing, but still the best of me.'

She got up then and put her hand on his shoulder. He knew without knowing it, really, that this was the end, that something was accomplished that had had to be accomplished in both of them, and it was both a beginning and an end.

'Yes, you must go,' she said, 'because,' she said, resting against the window sill so that he would not know that she was reeling, 'because I am a little tired.'

He sensed that a loud noise, even a word, even his own voice charged as it was with feeling might break something in this room. He did not dare say good-bye. But at the door he turned and looked back. She was standing at the window holding onto the curtain.

It is strange, she thought, that now I am not afraid of dying. There was no longer anything to be done. In spite of the whirl of pain that already possessed her head and drove her to the bed to lie down, in spite of it and beyond it was a great clarity and peace.

Chapter Nine

MARK waited at his hotel all day, not daring to go out. He waited without knowing exactly why he was waiting, going over the last few minutes in his mind, seeing Doro standing at the window and wondering what had made him feel so strongly that he must go at just that moment, hardly saying good-bye.

In the evening a message was delivered to him, an envelope addressed in a strange hand. It was a note from Claire. He did not dare read it. He sat on the bed with the letter in his hand not daring to guess what was in it. The things that one knows already are the hardest to hear. It was to say that Doro had had one of her dizzy spells and was in bed. He wasn't to worry, but she would be unable to see him again until the summer, when the school year would be over. She would need all her strength to get through it.

The envelope was full of rose petals, which she must have slipped in as she could not see to hold a pen. She would write later and he must send her his address.

Mark sat with his head in his hands feeling as if he were splitting up into a hundred different voices, all speaking at once. He must let them talk, must let them scream and sob for a while. There was nothing to do, he knew, but wait for this chaos of emotion to resolve itself: the voice which said: 'This is your fault. You have made her ill.' The voice which said: 'The terrible thing is to be able to do nothing, to be here and to be able to do nothing, especially not to let her guess how horrible it is to be able to do nothing. You must disappear. You must cease to exist as a reality, as someone who will come running up the path.' The voice which said: 'My love, my love, my love, why have you left me alone?' These voices he knew came from no deep place. They were like flashes of lightning in a thunderstorm. They did not have anything to do with the sky above. Everything they said to him would pass away in time to reveal what they did not say, which would be the truth.

In time he lay down on his bed looking at the ceiling curiously, a splotch of brown — a leak in the roof, no doubt. As he began to observe the marks on the ceiling, gradually the inner agitation, the troubled surface of his mind, grew quiet. One by one the voices were silenced. He thought of that last conversation. The thing he could do for her, the whole meaning of their relationship, he saw would lie in his work. And there is so much to do, he thought. There is so much to do that I must begin at once. Where there is action possible there can be no despair.

The loneliness would come later. It is harder to get beyond it. But in the end he would come to see that one does not find this kind of love, built on understanding, and ever lose it. It would not matter now where he was, she would always be there. It was a way of living he had found. It was the means of living, not with her, but with himself.